No More Secrets

2QT PUBLISHING

First Edition published 2023 by

2QT Limited (Publishing)

Settle, North Yorkshire BD24 9RH United Kingdom

Printed in Great Britain by IngramSpark

A CIP catalogue record for this book is available
from the British Library

ISBN 978-1-914083-79-2

No More Secrets

FRANK ENGLISH

Secrets Revealed

Poppy sat in her study in her cottage, a half-written page on her desk before her, and a faraway look in her eyes as she gazed out of the little window into the indeterminate distance over the fields and woods. Her second romantic novel was close to conclusion. But continuing bouts of reminiscence and nostalgia periodically interrupted her story flow. She couldn't help but think about her two dearest friends that no longer spent time in her company.

Two years had passed since that dreadful day when her closest friend and associate, Florence, passed from the gloriously wonderful experiences and adventures they had shared. She missed her company dreadfully. She missed the friendship they had shared since they were eight years old, that memorable Christmas at Boulders Wood when they shared a room and founded their close friendship.

Her other close friend, George Garside, had lost Florence as his wife in childbirth when she was experiencing a miscarriage, alone, without him near. The last thing Poppy had heard from George was his plea to allow him access to her should he need her support. That request came at the gathering for afternoon tea at the funeral.

She missed him desperately. Why had he not called when she was open to his visits? Still, life couldn't be frozen in limbo, and she owed it to herself to pursue her ambitions to their ultimate conclusions.

The front door opened slowly, encouraging Poppy to walk through to the sitting room, knowing that whoever had just entered was allowed to be there as only a key would grant entry. In the middle of the sitting room, of all people, stood … George.

"I knew you would come as soon as you were ready," she said quietly, as they embraced. "I knew it."

"I had to be sure it was you I really wanted," he acknowledged, holding her tightly to him. "I had to be sure I really wanted to spend the rest of my life with you, now that I can devote all my time to the woman I really love and have done so all my life."

"Yes, I will, my George," Poppy said confidently. "I *will* marry you."

"At last," he sighed deeply. "At last!"

And so it continues…

CHAPTER I

"Have you heard the astounding news?" Poppy's father, Tommy Spence, uttered with a good deal of urgency, as he rushed into her cottage out of heavy and blustery showers.

"No, Father," Poppy said as she replaced deliberately her ink-laden writing quill into its holder on her desk before rising to hug him. "What's so urgent that we can't exchange our usual pleasantries? Now, a hug if you please."

"This," he explained, handing her the front cover of the Times, after the hug from his daughter. "Apparently, *The Illustrated London News* and *The London Evening News* were the first to publish. This grave occurrence obviously then spread like the proverbial wildfire."

"My goodness!" she gasped after looking at the newspaper's full, black-bordered front page with its image of Queen Victoria at its centre, and a stark headline proclaiming in bold black capitals.

DEATH OF THE QUEEN

"I know she's been unwell for a while, but … this is so … incomprehensible. What will happen now? Will it herald the end of the monarchy in this country?"

"I don't think so," her father assured her. "Her eldest son will become King Edward VII, I should imagine. Apparently, she died at six thirty in the evening at Osborne House on the Isle of Wight where she loved to stay and had been doing so for quite some time."

"But isn't he a bit … old for such a thing?" Poppy insisted. "Bearing in mind his Mama was eighty-one and had been on the throne since she was eighteen."

"They will have to follow protocol, I think, no matter how old he is," Tommy replied with a grin and an almost dismissive shrug. "He's about sixty, I believe, although I don't follow matters to do with royalty too closely, really. I don't think they will be letting me know personally or seeking my advice any time soon."

"Father!" she gasped, but burst into a knowing giggle, being used to his sense of humour which had ripened over the last few years since his second child had been born. "How are Little Annie and Arthur today, and Sally, of course?"

"As nippers always are – full of beans and unbridled energy," he gasped, wiping imaginary sweat from his furrowed brow. "And Sally is … Sally, my beautiful wife and a gloriously wonderful mother.

"And you, Poppy, how are *you*?" Tommy continued after a moment's thought. "How is your latest book doing?"

"It's going to the publisher before too much longer," Poppy explained with a satisfied grin. "Jenny Wilton, my publisher, thinks it is wonderfully gripping."

"What's it going to be called?" Tommy asked, excited to hear that great success might be hers at last.

"It's a title that Florence had taken and completed only a tythe of the total number of chapters needed to set it on its way," Poppy acknowledged. "George has allowed me to take on the story and mould it into my own style. It is to be called *Faithfully Yours*, and it's a romance."

⁓

"Could you get that, Old Chap?" Jonas Jamieson asked Toby because of the interminably loud banging at the front door. "I don't know who might be calling at this time of evening, but you need to be careful. You don't know what criminals are about these days."

Toby and Jenny were still overwhelmed by the opulence of the house's interior Jonas had managed to purchase in the better part of Richmond in Yorkshire's North Riding. He had promised Jenny Bott that she wouldn't regret agreeing to moving in with him, and he certainly had delivered on his promise. Polished wooden doors fitted with shiny brass hinges and handles, expensively exotic embossed wall coverings, carpets to all floors, along with the latest in furniture – including *real*, comfortable beds in which to sleep in all five bedrooms. Jenny and her son Toby had never even *seen* such things let alone lived with all this stuff surrounding them.

"My word! Mi Lady!" Jonas said as Jenny entered the living room bearing a mahogany tray upon which sat silver service tea pot with steaming spout, bone China crockery bearing buttered scones and slices of Victoria sponge cake. "You have the air of a lady of the manor about you, my dear."

"But you can't come barging in here!" Toby's voice ricocheted off the hallway walls. "Now go—"

"Close your mouth, lad!" a gruff authoritarian voice interrupted the boy as its owner flung open the living room door causing it to rebound from the wall as its hinges protested. "We can and ... we have, Jonas Jamieson. We have a warrant here for your arrest on the counts of robbery, attempted rape and attempted murder."

"I have no idea what you are talking about, Old Chap," Jonas retorted. "So, you can—"

"You will have the opportunity to plead your case at the police station where you will be questioned," newly promoted Inspector Shaw snapped. "I would suggest your lady might be advised to contact your legal representative as soon as maybe, but you will be spending the next twenty-four hours at least in the cells. Take him!"

Three burly police officers wrestled him out of his bath-chair much to his discomfort and complaints.

"You'll be sorry for this indignity, constable," Jonas warned. "Once my barrister hears of it—"

"He will be granted access," the policeman said roughly, "and it's *Inspector* Shaw to you, young man."

Young Toby was brushed out of the way unceremoniously as he tried to intervene to protect his master, and Jenny could only stand and watch with her hand over her mouth, a look of abject fear in her eyes.

"Don't worry Jenny dear," Jonas shouted as he was bundled into the horse-drawn Black Maria. "I'll be back soon. They have no real evidence to show anything, and my—"

The rear doors of the police wagon slammed shut, cutting off anything further he tried to utter. The glorious shiny shires started their journey to the police cells with their prisoner still protesting his innocence inside.

A genteel tapping at the front door of Poppy and George Garside's cottage stopped her and her father in mid-sentence. Aware of the problems that had been forced upon his daughter in times gone by in that abode, Tommy Spence sprang from his chair to make his way to the door. As it was forged in a significantly more secure fashion because louts and ruffians had forced their way in before, Tommy had no way of seeing who was behind its now formidable barrier.

Opening it carefully to the full extent of its short security chain, he couldn't help but see that the caller would certainly be no threat.

"Jenny Wilton, I presume?" he greeted the well-dressed young woman the other side of the threshold as he removed the obstacles to his opening the door fully. "Please come in."

"Dr Spence," she replied as he led her into the sitting room. "It's so good to see you once again."

"I must away now Poppy my dear," he went on. "Calls to make in the line of duty, I'm afraid."

He embraced his daughter, with the promise to visit her later in the week, and then made for his small coach and pair to be off on his rounds.

"So lovely to see you, Poppy," Jenny offered with a smile as she divested and occupied the easy chair just vacated by Poppy's father. "You are so lucky to be able to spend time with your father on a regular basis."

"He calls in two or three times a week to check that everything is all right," Poppy explained. "I am lucky also that I have my George here most of the time, and my Uncle Ross lives just up the driveway in Boulders Wood's main house. They are the ones that rescued me a couple of times from ruffians who broke into this cottage to threaten me a while ago now."

"My goodness!" Jenny gasped, looking over her shoulder to make sure the outside door had been secured. "They caused you no harm I assume?"

"Two out of the three were incapacitated – one of them by Abigail as it happens – while the other was flattened by my George," Poppy said with a nod and a smile.

"By petite Abigail McIntyre? *Our* little Abigail?" Jenny gasped. "How could that be?"

"She understood we were being broken into and took immediate action to incapacitate the lead attacker with a swipe across the head with a handy brass poker," Poppy re-joined with a contented smile. "The rest was sorted out by George and Ross."

"We now have a window of opportunity for your new book," Jenny advised once she had taken her first sip of hot tea from her steaming cup that Poppy had provided, to be followed by a nibble of Victoria sponge cake.

"I don't understand," Poppy queried. "What do you mean by 'window of opportunity'?"

"I have been able to arrange for one of the larger publishing houses to lend a hand to get the book released within the next week or two," she replied with a twinkle in her eye and a slight frisson of excitement coursing her frame.

"That sounds exciting!" Poppy exclaimed, putting down her cup and saucer before she dropped it. "However, do I detect the appearance of that mischievous word ... 'but'?"

"Not such a *bad* thing, really," Jenny explained. "The manuscript has to be in full and correct order by ... the day after tomorrow."

"Ouch!" Poppy winced, a look of mock hurt lurking around her face.

"Is that a problem?" Jenny asked, genuinely concerned.

"No problem at all," her friend assured her. "I have all but finished the typing and all I need to do is to check it through, which I have done five times already. So, my dear Jenny, tomorrow it will be in your fair hands."

"No pressure then?" Jenny giggled, excited by their new venture into the unknown.

"Are you allowed to tell me which publisher it will be floating off to?" Poppy asked, almost not daring to hope.

"No names – just yet, but it's a big one," Jenny said slowly. "And you will be as excited as I am."

—⁓—

Heavy with the acridly pungent stench of stale urine, rancid body odours and nauseatingly stinking unclean breath hanging in the air due to the lack of ventilation, the dishevelled and raggily unclean, almost lifeless forms of eight males crowded the room. Police cells were never designed to be comfortable and inviting as precursors to whatever an almost inevitable stretch in prison might bring.

Having had his request for an individual cell refused several times, and the demand for medical attention ignored, Jonas Jamieson's badly injured knee had become grossly infected, and his body ravaged with almost unbearable pain.

"I say, Old Chap," he shouted as he rattled the bars of what seemed to be an interminable prison, "is there any chance I might be shipped off to an infirmary?"

"Infirmary?" a quieter voice asked from the furthest dark corner of the cell. "Why? What's up wi' thi?"

"Nothing to concern you, my good man," Jonas reacted patronisingly. "I don't think you'll be able to help."

"Patronising as ever, eh Mr … Jonas Jamieson?" another hidden voice returned a little more sternly.

"Who are *you*?" Jonas challenged, concerned that this newcomer might be linked to someone that might bear him a grudge. He had no idea who it might be, but should he be concerned? "Do I know you?"

"You certainly won't know *me*, but I know people that most certainly do know *you*," the voice retaliated sharply.

"As in…?" Jonas puzzled, more than a little perturbed at his rejoinder.

"I take it you *do* remember the Thresher Hall job?" the voice jibed. "You know, the distribution of the proceeds from the … sale?"

"What if I do?" Jonas snorted, not feeling quite as brave as he did. "That was—"

"Crooked and devious I believe are the terms," his jouster returned. "Enough to cause joy in the heart of the Big Man? I feel sure he would love to be made aware of the sharp deals that were done, and who it was did him out of all that money. Catch my drift?"

"Don't you try to—!" Jonas blustered, believing he might be able to wriggle his way out of what seemed to be a rather large threat growing.

"I know a certain … George Garside … as well, and I believe he would be more than happy to hear of his old enemy's dire demise at the hands of some 'friends' of mine," the mystery voice threatened.

"Oy! Pack it in!" the guard's rough, deep voice boomed from the door. "Or you *will* be sorry."

"I need to see the doctor because of my severely injured knee," Jonas's whispered rasp barely broke the silence in return. "Is there no compassion out there?"

"What you are feeling *now* is the least of your worries," another deeper and more threatening voice ruptured the gathering unrest. "I should watch my back if I were you … 'Old Chap'. See you around."

CHAPTER 2

Breakfast was always early at Wisteria Cottage as George's day generally started when his children awoke demanding to be fed and watered. At three years of age, they played noisily, were closely into mischief and argued a good deal with each other.

They always slept and breakfasted at Wisteria Cottage with their father and Poppy who had only recently tentatively set their wedding day, largely because George was too busy to take off time from his intensive work with the farm's livestock. Sally's father, Jim, was a canny manager but even he couldn't cope on his own without help.

After breakfast, Alice and her twin sister were usually taken to their granny by their father to be looked after until George collected them when he had finished work. This was an arrangement that allowed Poppy to write, George to work and Lilly to indulge her passion of being with her grandchildren.

"I'm a little concerned," Poppy said to her George when he had returned from settling his nippers with his mother. They usually spent a precious half hour together before he attacked his pile of papers in the office, they had set up in the room that Florence had used as her writing room.

He spent no more than half an hour there, considering it to be a necessary evil of overall management of the farm, before leaving for what was the secondary love of his life – hands on with the animals.

"Not us, I hope?" he grimaced, accepting full well that he did spend an inordinate amount of time away from his beloved Poppy, as he pulled on his coat. "We *will* be married soon and…"

"No, my lovely man," she assured him with a loving smile. "Nothing to do with you … except in a roundabout sort of a way."

"I don't understand," he responded, shaking his head slightly.

"I've been speaking to your sisters Charity and Florence, who seem to believe that your mother has been doing and saying strange things since your father's burial," Poppy said quietly.

"And by that you mean?" George asked, more than a little perturbed.

"They didn't elucidate," she returned with a shrug, "and I can't even hazard a guess. Perhaps you need to speak to them to find out precisely what they mean?"

"I'll speak to them when I collect Alice and Maisie," he replied quickly. "Have to be away, my dearest. New stock coming in, so I need to help Jim Smallshore to get 'em in and catalogued. See you later this afternoon."

"Don't forget that you said you would look into employing more staff, so you don't have to work so hard," Poppy reminded him. "Don't forget also that Sally restarts in the dairy tomorrow, part-time…"

A vigorous nod of the head, a pointing of his forefinger and a knowing smile signalled his leaving, to be followed by a snick of the self-locking front door.

Poppy sighed reasonably contentedly as she sided away the usual crockery and aimed for her study. About to enter to take up her writing again, she was stopped in her tracks by the sound of a key trying with difficulty to usher its wielder into the cottage. Turning slowly with more than a little apprehension she watched the inner door to the vestibule open very slowly…

⌒

"This is not justice!" Jonas complained as a policeman brought in a bowlful of slops to eat. "And this is not proper food! I'm not eating that! … Ouch!"

He fell to the floor, dazed, after a heavy blow to the back of the head. The policeman saw what had happened, but turned away and locked the outer door to the cells as he left.

"I warned you … Old Chap," a deeply raspy voice hissed as Jonas hit the floor again, unconscious from the beating he had just received. "The Boss Man knows you are here and understands perfectly well that your present lifestyle could not be sustained other than with a huge influx of cash that you don't have the means to acquire. You probably can't hear or see me now," the voice continued with a wheezy rasp. "What a shame that your ears and eyes seem to have become injured and swollen. You must be careful not to walk into … anything in future. Guard!"

Almost on cue the cell door clanged open as a policeman and two hospital-attired orderlies clattered in, bearing a dishevelled stretcher upon which they bundled a badly injured Jonas Jamieson, almost as if they knew what to expect.

"I have to ask what happened to him, but I can probably guess the answer already," Inspector Shaw sighed as the body was loaded unceremoniously into the back of a horse-drawn hospital van. "Richmond Cottage Hospital sharpish, and you, Constable Baines, hop in and make sure he doesn't escape, though I believe there will be little chance of that in his state."

"Smithson!" he shouted to another of his constables as he sank into the chair behind his desk. "In here! Now!"

"Sir?" a shifty-looking, uniformed policeman slunk around his door.

"Close the door and come here," the inspector ordered brusquely. "How did all this happen?"

"All what, Sir?" the subordinate asked, a seemingly innocent puzzled look decorating his face.

"You know perfectly well!" the inspector growled. "And if you don't, I'll make sure that not only your life here won't be worth living, but you won't find any sort of a job anywhere else. Now, speak."

The young officer spoke haltingly about what he thought could have happened, but equally seriously about his ignorance of who in – or out – the cells might have arranged it.

"Here's the thing," Shaw went on. "I know you live in the area with your wife and family. True?"

"Yes, Sir," the constable replied defensively. "Lived here all my life."

"How would you like a transfer to York?" the inspector suggested pointedly. "Travelling every day or … moving your family to somewhere new?"

"Sir?" the subordinate asked, almost on a hoarse whisper.

"All I need is a name," the inspector insisted bluntly.

The door to her sitting room opened slowly, with Poppy not knowing whom to expect as she backed off towards the kitchen.

"Jenny!" she gasped as her friend slid around the door. "You frightened me to death because it seemed like the front door was being forced open."

"I put the key in upside-down, I'm very sorry to say," Jenny responded. "It wasn't until I had tried it a time or two that I realised my mistake. Anyway, we're here now."

"We?" Poppy puzzled before her dear friend walked in. "Abigail! I didn't expect *you*."

They all embraced, pleased to be together again after such a long time.

"I'd like you to meet Peter Olleranshaw," Jenny explained, as a man she had never seen before, entered quietly. "Your new publisher."

Poppy's mouth very slowly began to open in awe and surprise to see this tall, bearded, good-looking middle-aged man whose imposing stature almost stopped her breathing.

"New publisher?" Poppy said, the confusion obvious in her flushed face. "But I thought…?"

"Peter and I have set up a business partnership to draw on the publishing expertise of a significant number of publishing houses," Jenny explained excitedly. "Peter has been in the business for quite some time and has a wide range of contacts that could prove to be game-changing."

"And how are you, Mr Olleranshaw, going to make a difference to how women are viewed as writers?" Poppy asked bluntly. "We all know it's definitely not a female writer's world, especially if we don't change our name to suggest male influence."

"The publisher I work with is definitely not one of those," Peter assured her.

"Is *he* a *woman*, then?" she retorted pointedly.

"No, but he does believe that women writers at the very least are as intuitive and creative as their male counterparts," he returned confidently without being defensive. "In fact, I believe you need to drop the pretence of being a notional male, and continue your writing under your own name, Poppy Spence. No need for the initials to try to hide your true identity."

Poppy fell silent, not sure what to say, or how to cope with such almost brutal honesty.

"You have made a moderate success, I understand, as P.P.Spence?" he continued. "From what I hear from Jenny, this new book, with the author's name as *Poppy* Spence, will exceed all expectations, and stands a very good chance of being moderately successful."

"You'll need a copy of my manuscript, then?" she returned, almost daring him to say no.

"Indeed, I will be taking a copy with me to work tomorrow," he said confidently. "You do have a copy handy?"

Poppy left the room quickly, to return moments later with a large foolscap-sized package, saying as she thrust it into his hands. "This big enough?"

"Not concerned about the size," he countered. "It's what it has to say that matters. If it grabs and captivates me almost immediately and maintains its grip throughout, it will do. Now I must away as I have a lot of reading to do before tomorrow."

With the manuscript tucked safely under his arm, he turned quickly on his highly polished heels, bidding them all farewell, and marched out to his carriage on the crunchy driveway.

"Well!" Poppy gasped. "Business-like, if nothing else. Abigail? Jenny?"

"I could see by your face and initial silence that you were … captivated by his appearance at least," Abigail observed. "How *is George* these days, by the way?"

"Broken nose and cheek bone, loss of several teeth, cracked femur and, we believe, there might be internal damage," the hospital doctor observed, noticing that his patient was barely aware of what he was saying. "Mr Jamieson? Can you hear me?"

A slow, mumbled splutter responded to his question, as blood oozed from his battered mouth, swollen gums and badly disfigured nose, before total silence enveloped his being.

"Not a pleasant sight," the doctor muttered to the policeman. "A long and slow crawl back to some semblance of normality, though the strong likelihood of more to come if his sentence is on the horizon. He'll have to stay here at least until his trial."

"But—? The policeman butted in.

"No buts, my man," the doctor checked him. "The system is here to punish and change, but not to the detriment of his living some sort of a reasonably normal life after the judicial system has taken its pound of flesh."

"That means I'll have to stay here as well," the constable muttered through clenched teeth. "Now who's being punished?"

"Part of the job, I presume?" the doctor responded through a benign smile. "Part of the job."

"But will he survive long enough to stand – or sit – for a trial?" the constable asked, as if it meant anything to him.

"*That* will have to be seen," came the doctor's sharp reply as he made to leave the room. "It's in the Lord's hands for now."

Chapter 3

"George?" Poppy asked her man over tea the second Sunday in April of the year of the Queen's passing.

"Yes, my lovely," he replied, sitting back at the table in his mahogany chair. "What can I do you for?"

"Do you remember the question I asked you not so long ago?" she went on.

"And which of the ten million questions you usually ask, was that one?" he smiled, feeling a little smug for having disarmed her usually unexplained question that could have led him in any direction he had forgotten about.

"A very important but obviously easily forgotten one that you agreed to consider some seven months ago," she responded with a coldly sarcastic tone.

"Was it the one about having a … holiday in Scarborough in the summer?" he said a little uncomfortably. "Or—?"

"Not even close!" she replied without lifting her face from her writing table. "And neither will any of your *magical* questions be."

Silence descended, until she uttered with a mixture of triumph and finality, "You promised to employ somebody to take over more of *your* duties, so we could take time off together to … do something … interesting once in a while. Have you?"

"Well," he began his answer, "as it turns out, I have a young Scottish chap coming to see me tomorrow. He *seems* to have the right credentials and experience, and he seems to be raring to go. If everything goes all right tomorrow, we'll set him on for a week or two to see how things pan out. Experienced folks are few and far between these days. Ross and I have agreed to put him through his paces."

"I hope it turns out good, because we don't seem to have had much time together, and…" she paused for a moment before carrying on, "…and we need to find time for our wedding day. You do still *want* to marry me, don't you?"

"An unnecessary question, my lovely," he replied, getting up to draw her to him. "The answer to which you already know.

"Of course, I want to marry you," he assured her, drawing a genuine smile to her lips. "Once we have yonder fellow in harness, we can plan it as a matter of some urgency."

Their conversation was interrupted by an urgent rattling at the front door, causing Poppy to start and her man to frown at its interruption.

"Who the—?" he muttered as he headed towards the sound. "All right! All right! I'm coming. Don't knock the door in!"

Once open, the door bounced back on its hinges as George's sister, Florence, barged in.

"Steady lass, steady," George urged as she almost ricocheted off her brother. "What's the rush? Has somebody died?"

"You need to come home quickly!" she gasped, out of breath from running from Garside Farm. "There's been an … accident. One of the twins—"

George heard nothing else, as he charged out of the bungalow, feet not touching the ground, his hair streaming in the early spring breeze. The air hereabouts was beginning to warm very slowly after a sharp winter where heavy falls of thick snow had made life somewhat difficult. The most recent snows had begun to disappear, leaving uneven piles of darkening ice, making it hard to get about.

"What's happened?" Poppy asked, quietly concerned, once Florence had sat down to regain both strength and breath. "One of the twins…?"

"They were chasing about in the field around a skittish group of cows," Florence started to explain as a well of tears in each eye corner gathered and threatened to burst. "One of the cows knocked Alice over with a kick to the chest, sending her unconscious. I don't know about her condition, but it sounds serious."

Flinging her coat over her shoulders, Poppy made for the door, with Florence in hot pursuit. Not having been outside for a day or two, Poppy gasped as the cold air caught her breath, making her wrap her coat around her more closely. Although only a short walk from the Boulders Wood main house, the scattered and disparate piles of ice and snow, made for poor, slow progress.

The doctor's pony trap was already at the house door. As they entered the front room, George could be seen pacing the room with his daughter clutched closely to his chest as he uttered the words, "No! No! No!" slowly, quietly and with tears streaming down his cheeks.

Apologising profusely, the doctor collected his instruments and bag together and made for the open door, as he threw over his shoulder, "I'll bring the death certificate by the end of the week."

"What is it, George?" Poppy asked, putting her hand on his shoulder. "Is the—?"

"She's gone, Poppy. She's gone," he replied, a desperate sob in his throat. "Mother had let them out when the cows were in the field, and Alice was trampled to death. Her sister, Maisie, is in deep shock, and won't respond to anyone."

"What's happened?" a deeply resonant voice filled the room. "I called to see George about yonder herd in the north field, and everyone's in here. No work today?"

"Alice has had an accident with that north field herd," Poppy explained. "She's been trampled and—"

"My God!" Ross gasped. "Why—?"

"Mother let the twins out to play, and they wandered into the field where the herd was ruminating," Florence explained, tears coursing her cheeks. "Alice got too close to one of the cows which kicked out, caught her in the chest and knocked her onto the floor. By the time someone got to her, her heart had stopped, and she couldn't be brought round."

"Mother has been behaving very strangely lately," Charity warned. "Forgetful, staring into the distance as if trying to find Dad, and seeming not to understand where she is or what to do."

"She doesn't seem to know that Alice is ... not here anymore," Florence butted in. "And I am sure she would not understand what she has done either."

"What next, then?" Ross asked, although he thought he might be able to guess from what happened when *his* mother had spiked Old Joss during *his* attack on Poppy as a nipper.

~

"It looks like amputation above the knee might be the only way not to lose the whole leg," the doctor explained to a battered and bruised Jonas Jamieson.

"And what might that entail?" the injured man muttered with difficulty through a swollen and painful mouth, blood seeping from the battered gums where his teeth used to be.

"General anaesthetic so you have no idea that your leg is leaving your body," the doctor said. "We then do an excellent job of embroidery to keep the rest of your limbs intact. Then, lots of bed rest either in hospital or in the prison's medical facility."

"Do I have a choice?" Jonas spluttered.

"What? Between life and death?" the doctor uttered starkly.

"I'm being done for petty larceny, not for murder," the young man complained.

"Simply explaining what the likely outcome would be if you left a gangrenous limb to fester without offering the best redress for your sort of injury," the doctor butted in with a shrug. "*That* is your choice. If you don't want to go ahead with this life-saving operation, fine. But you will be moved immediately to prison to await trial – with no help from us – and you know what *that* means. You'll probably get six to twelve months with hard labour, and with *your* leg, that could be life-threatening from another perspective."

"Left with no choice, then, Old Chap?" Jonas spluttered again, shrugging his shoulders with hopelessness. "Will I be able to stay here in the meantime? I mean, in the general population, in that filth and degradation I might as well give up."

"If you agree to the operation, you *will* stay here until the operation is complete," the doctor explained calmly. "It will take a further two months to make sure your leg is on the mend properly before you can be considered for prison. So, you will be sentenced in absentia, to fulfil your prison sentence within a month or two thereafter."

"How will I get about after that?" Jonas asked, beginning to understand the seriousness of his situation at last.

"Crutches mainly," the doctor offered. "Or the bathchair you have been using up to now. You could have a wooden leg fitted once the wound is properly healed, probably within twelve months. I will arrange matters with Inspector Shaw tomorrow."

"Happy days!" Jonas replied with a stifled grimace. "Watch out George Garside. Your time will come, have no doubt, and when it does, I shall be there to gloat."

"You have visitors to see you, Jamieson," his police guard called, drawing the prisoner out of his gloating reverie. "Five minutes, and no more."

He ushered two people into the small hospital room, one of whom sat on a chair while the younger one stood behind.

"Jenny! Toby!" Jonas exclaimed, glad to see them. "How good to see you both!"

"Good gracious!" Jenny Bott gasped. "You look in a sorry mess, and no mistake. We had come to see if you were still alive. What's going to happen now?"

"Well, Old Girl, it seems that if I want to live, I will have to lose half of the leg," he said slowly. "Small price to pay I think, because it seems like my court hearing may well deliver me into Edward's prison for a month or two on the lesser charge of theft."

"My God! Can't they do anything to save your leg?" she retorted. "Bind it and cure it, perhaps?"

"'Fraid not, Old Bean," he said. "Gangrene can be a killer for which the only cure is to remove as much of the offending appendage as possible. Two things I'd like to ask you both?"

"Anything, Master!" Toby butted in quickly. "Whatever you need, you only have to ask."

"And what might that be?" Jenny asked, a little more cynically. "*What* do we have to do?"

"For you Toby, my boy," Jonas went on. "I should like you to look after your mother, and—"

"And what do *I* have to do?" Jenny Bott asked, a little more warily.

"All you have to do, Old Girl, is to promise to … marry me when I get out of this hole," he added with a shrug and a gentle squeeze of her hand.

Both mother and son stood in dumbfounded silence, not knowing what answer to give to his last – very pointed – question.

"What would you say to becoming Mrs Jonas Jamieson, Jenny? Eh?" he said, urging her answer.

"Does that mean that I would become your … stepson?" Toby asked slowly.

"Indeed, it does, Toby my lad … if that is what you would like," Jonas responded gently. "Well, lovely lady? Jenny Bott, or Jenny Jamieson? Any preference?"

"Can I trust that your kindness will *continue*, though?" Jenny asked pointedly. "Would you honour and be eternally kind to me?"

He stopped for a few moments of deep thought before saying, "I will promise you that I will always be kind to you both and look after you to the best of my limited ability."

Here, self-deprecatingly, he swept his arm over his obvious short comings, as the doctor entered the room.

"Time to get started, Mr Jamieson," he urged. "Your wife and son need to leave now, to return within twenty-four hours."

"Tomorrow, then, my lovely?" Jonas suggested to his visitors, as they turned to leave. "O.K. doc? Got your sharp scissors ready?"

Two pairs of worried eyes looked at each other as the body-laden trolley made its way to the door to the operating theatre, ready for a very important two hours or so in Jonas's life.

"How could he take this so calmly, Mother?" Toby asked with a gasped wince. "Does he realise what is about to happen to him?"

"I think you'll find that he does," his mother replied with a knowing smile.

"And *will* you marry him?" Toby asked pointedly.

***

"It's called 'brain congestion' which is a combination leading to mania melancholia and hysteria," the doctor explained. "This leads to a desire to hide from society and is often called 'old-timers disease'."

"Does this mean she will have no idea what she is either doing or has done at any given time?" Ross Senior asked of the Harley Street medic.

"Exactly," the doctor replied. "Why do you ask? Has something happened that is inexplicable?"

"The mother of my granddaughter's young man allowed one of his very young twin daughters to wander away from her care into a field full of skittish cows," Nell explained. "She was trampled and died from her injuries. Granny Lilly neither knew where she had gone nor what had happened to her – and still doesn't."

"The name and understanding of this condition come from the research of Arnold Pick, a Czechoslovakian psychiatrist in the late 19th century, and talks of the 'Pick Body' in the brain," Dr Grant replied. "And there is nothing as yet that can be done to alleviate the condition."

"No cure, then?" Ross Senior asked, more in hope than in

reality, as they left the consulting room.

"Unfortunately … not," the medic said, closing the door behind them.

"What are we going to do, Ross?" Nell asked, knowing how they would have to make sure little Maisie didn't suffer her sister's demise.

"George will have to make some difficult decisions, I think," he answered. "So, we ought, perhaps, to offer some advice to make things easier for him and Poppy. Then I feel we ought to be on our way to the Mediterranean."

"Your chest getting worse for you?" Nell said, worried that things were moving too fast with his physical condition.

"Doctor considers we need to go sooner rather than later," he suggested as he burst into a serious bout of coughing.

Chapter 4

"And from here you will be taken to the House of Correction for the North Riding at Northallerton, and there you shall spend four months of imprisonment with hard labour – taking into account the length of time you have already spent in custody – and with no reprieve until your sentence is ended," the judge pronounced, to the gasps of Jenny Bott and her son, Toby.

"But, your honour, I—" Jonas butted in.

"Be careful, young man, or your sentence may be increased," the judge went on. "I have given you the minimum term of incarceration allowed by His Majesty's Court that you must follow with good grace and behaviour."

With that, he stood to leave to the usher's 'All rise!' and to the bustling of Jonas's body to the cells below the court room, in preparation for his incarceration. It would now be up to the governor of the facility at Northallerton, along with the intervention of the hospital doctor as to how this sentence was carried out.

In the public gallery sat a shadowy figure that took great interest in the proceedings, and a certain degree of satisfaction in the outcome of the trial. As satisfying was the onlooker's observation of Jonas's physical state which was as much to do with his actions as his stay in police cells. He sat back for a moment or two, a smile playing about his mouth corners as he watched Jonas's struggle to hop down the steps to the cells, ready to be shipped to prison.

He could imagine how his foppish treatment of his hard fellow prisoners would be greeted by them on the whole, with one and a half legs to try to maintain balance. At last! Justice!

<hr>

"We therefore commit this body to the ground … earth to earth; ashes to ashes; dust to dust; in sure and certain hope of the Resurrection to eternal life…"

George stood by the tiny grave opening as his beautiful little daughter's coffin slipped slowly into its final black resting place, taking what seemed like an eternity to disappear from sight. As she dropped away, his head bowed gradually and, as his eyes closed, tears rolled down his cheeks as if marking time with the coffin.

Poppy was by his side as ever, supporting arm around his waist, drawing him ever closer as she, too, wept in silent homage to his little Alice. Family only surrounded the grave – except for Grandma Lilly and Alice's twin, Maisie, who was too young to understand the loss of her sister. Aunt Lilly Victoria remained in the Garside home to look after both.

"Why are we sitting here, Lilly Victoria?" her mother demanded. "And where is everyone else? The young man, whatever his name is? The other little girl? Will she be back for dinner?"

She paused for a while, falling into silence, a definitely puzzled look invading her aged face.

"My husband? Where is my … husband?" Lilly continued. "I do have a husband … don't I? I haven't seen him for a while. His name is George…"

"George is your *son*," Lilly Victoria said gently. "Your husband was called Tom."

"Tom. Tom?" Lilly returned. "*Was* called Tom? Has he changed his name? What to? Harry? Barry? Larry?"

"No, Mama, he died a while ago," her daughter replied very cautiously, a tear beginning to glisten. "His heart gave out, here in this very bedroom."

"He can't be!" Lilly gasped. Almost immediately the look of shock on her face slid away as she said, "Is it time for dinner soon?"

She moved slowly to the kitchen and sat at the table with a bump and continued to drink her now cold cup of tea.

"Where is little Alice, Maisie?" her Nanna asked.

Maisie was taken aback somewhat by the question, but was sharp enough to answer, "She has gone to live with God and Jesus in heaven, Nanna. I miss her."

"But I saw your grandpa with her only this morning just after breakfast," Lilly explained, quite sharply. "So, she must be around. Go and find her, Maisie. I have something for you both."

Maisie turned to her aunt, a pleading look settling round her eyes, to which Lilly Victoria nodded towards the door for her to leave quickly before her nanna's questions became upsetting. By this time Lilly had headed upstairs again to her bedroom window to look for her granddaughter.

"There she is! Look, Lilly Victoria!" her mother called out, jabbing her finger towards the yard. "I told you so! She's with your father … What's his name?"

"Mother!" Lilly Victoria said, rounding on her sharply. "As I have told you several times already, Father died of a heart attack several years ago and he is no longer with us. Little Alice died when she was trampled by a herd of cows more than a week ago. Her funeral was today. Little Maisie, her sister, already has come to terms with that, and doesn't need reminding of it. So please accept the inevitable and don't upset her anymore."

"Oh…" Lilly Garside said lamely as she returned to her rocking chair by the bedroom window.

Leaving her mother looking out of the window, she regained the sitting room to discover her niece, Maisie, whom she found by the open front door sobbing, with tears streaming down her face.

"Maisie?" Lilly Victoria said softly as she caught up with her and drew her to her bosom to try to soothe her pain. "Come on now. Alice wouldn't want you to continue being upset. She—"

"But I *miss* her, Auntie Lilly Victoria," the little girl sobbed. "She's always in my head, and I see her in my mind all the time, from when I saw her being knocked over to now. I miss her so much."

As the family began to troop through the door, a few with raised eyebrows wanting to know what was happening, Lilly Victoria nodded her answer to their unspoken question about Maisie. Charity and sister Florence climbed the stairs to see to their mother, as George, Poppy and the rest of the extended family entered into the sombre living room.

"Quick! George!" Charity's panic-stricken voice echoed down the stairwell. "It's Mother! We think she has … gone!"

"Well then, Mr Kiss-Mi-Arse Jamieson, welcome to your new home," a familiar voice greeted him as he was wheeled into the House of Correction for the North Riding. "I feel sure you will be … welcomed … into your new abode for the next few months. Please make yourself at home."

Jonas grunted with displeasure and defiance at finding himself in this hell hole of a dungeon facility where he would have to stay for part of his sentence.

"Only staying for a couple of nights, Old Chap," Jonas explained to the prison guard. "I have to return to the charge of the doctor at Richmond Cottage Hospital for further treatment."

"Oh, haven't you heard?" the warder pointed out, a sly grin sliding into his face. "Doctor Smith has been transferred to a hospital near York, and his replacement has crossed you off his list. He has refused to treat a 'dangerous convict' when other God-fearing patients need him."

"But that can't be true!" he exclaimed, not believing his sneered suggestion. "I have to have treatment for my leg."

"Just got to know this morning," the warder scoffed, pleased that he had got one over on this annoying upstart. He knew already that he would be in for a hard time; his cell mates would make sure of that. But his attitude towards Jenny Bott and her son was a new and unforeseen departure for Jonas. Enlightened self-interest was perhaps the initial reaction to his having these sorts of feelings for her, but she had now become a special person, bringing out the best in his character that had lain dormant for many years which now, at last, was beginning to resurface.

Although off on the wrong foot initially, she had grown on him, with her svelte body and soft skin, beautiful blue eyes and gentle touch. How could he not have fallen for her? Only time would tell whether she would accept his offer, although he felt she knew how much of a difference the money he had gleaned would make to their life together.

The only problems he could foresee were his disabilities and the time he was to spend in prison.

"Well, Jonas Jamieson – Old Chap – it's good to see you back," a dark voice warned the young man that it was still there, sidling out of the recesses of his mind, causing him to wince internally. "I hope you are keen to meet your … acquaintances once again. They are certainly looking forward to meeting you! It's such a shame about your leg. See you later…"

The door to his cell clanged shut behind him as he plumped his severely aching body onto his less than comfortable prison bed where the covers didn't seem to have been washed this side of the last century. Blood and faecal stains lay in abundance on his dirty grey sheet, and the bed itself couldn't have been more uncomfortably hard than if it had been chiselled out of the rock upon which the prison had been built. Casting one last despairing look around this dingy hole, he slumped back and buried his face in his dirt encrusted hands in despair.

The rasping of key in rusty lock jerked him out of an uneasy slumber of vividly startling nightmares, making him feel his tormentors had returned to seek the satisfaction of inflicting further pain upon his already tortured body.

"Mr Jamieson?" the gentle voice called him. It was the Governor. "Collect your non-existent belongings and follow me…"

"Where are you taking me, Sir?" Jonas asked hesitantly, his mind still fogged by the unpleasant images that occupied it. He reached for his crutches and stumbled after the Governor in an ungainly shambolic fashion, cracking his knuckles on the metal, barred door in his haste not to be shut in again.

There were no guards to be seen as he tried to keep up with his guide who was by now waiting by the outside wall, holding the door to the outside world ajar. A significantly fearful look on his face indicated his puzzlement to the man before him.

"Don't concern yourself, Mr Jamieson," the Governor assured him. "We are not having a jail break. You are free to go."

Outside in the street stood a young woman holding open a carriage door, beckoning him to hurry.

"Jenny?" he gasped as he stumbled up the carriage steps and collapsed onto the seat, passing out as he hit the cushioned bench.

Jenny sat quietly by Jonas's bed at home watching him tossing and turning restlessly, a gasped groan escaping his tortured body periodically. She was relieved occasionally by her son who was severely concerned that his master might not survive the following twenty-four hours.

"Is he going to … die, Mam?" the lad asked his mother quietly concerned. Jonas had been good to him, treating him like his own son, and so he didn't want to lose him. Whatever needed to be done, Toby was prepared to do, so everything could be all right from now on.

"Jenny," a weakly quiet voice gasped. "Are you there, my lovely?"

"I'm here," she replied as she reached over to take his hand in hers. "How are you feeling?"

"Like something a wild pig has dumped in the undergrowth," he growled. "I'll survive though. Why have I been released when I should have had at least another three months to go on my sentence?"

"Never mind now," she answered. "I'll explain later."

"Tell me now!" he snapped. "Please?"

"It appears you have friends in high places, my dear," she began to explain, "who paid off your debt to *this* society. That's all I know, so relax and get well. If you do, you'll be up and about before long."

"Hopping about in no time, eh?" he said through a wheezy laugh and cough as he spat blood into a reasonably clean towel.

Not off on such a good start with this man, she was convinced now that he had significant feelings for her and her son. Was it because he needed someone to look after him in his parlous state, or were those apparent sentiments more deeply felt? Only time would tell. In the meantime, her present living conditions were the best she had experienced in her ever so short life. She would not be asking about the source of his – their – soon-found wealth, or how long it might last. She had never felt such security before, or the degree of self-confidence that it had brought. Hopefully it would last, giving them a much better standard of living than they had previously experienced.

Cynically pragmatic, she had to keep him alive for all their sakes, apart from her developing feelings for him. Would his attitude last or descend into sarcasm through everyday pressures, as had happened on many reasonably recent occasions? Why had he changed so obviously recently? Circumstance? Necessity? Her mind flooded with uncertainties, causing confusion and indecision.

"Do I detect feelings of uncertainty and doubt, my dear?" Jonas's strained voice butted quietly into the silence.

"How do you mean?" she said, with a briefly embarrassed pause.

"My change of … approach to you?" he replied. "I do have genuinely deep feelings for you – and for the lad, Toby here. Just let me get better and then I'll prove it to you. *Really*."

Chapter 5

"My God!" George wailed, gritting his teeth in pain and anguish, as he cast his angry glances to the heavens. "Haven't I suffered enough? First my little 'un and now, mi mam! What next?"

His mother was sitting in her rocking chair by the window in her bedroom. Eyes closed and hands clasped in her lap, as if taking a well-earned nap from her daily toils. A serene half smile seemed to grace her face like it had not done since her beloved husband's departure from her side. Officially husband he was not as they had never found the time to become joined legally. That didn't matter because it would have changed their lives only to make them financially poorer. However, the major consequence was that their four children were technically illegitimate.

Once again Poppy's arm drew him closer to convince him that she at least would always be there for him. Almost immediately a pair of little arms grasped him around the legs as a tiny tear-stained face looked up at his, pleading silently with him to lessen her anguish.

"Daddy?" she croaked, not really knowing what to say as *she* saw adult anguish in *his* face, too.

He picked her up and drew her to him, unable to bring appropriate words to mind to assuage her despair, sharing with her a profound feeling of emptiness.

A shocked sadness swept through the gathering as the other members of the Garside and McIntyre families poured into the bedroom.

"You all go downstairs while Joseph and I lay out her body for the doctor to examine and make the obvious pronouncements for legal reasons," Ross suggested. "A soothing cup of tea might not be such a bad idea."

***

"Natural causes as far as it is possible to tell," Doctor Twist suggested as he scribbled on his note pad in preparation for the drawing up of legal notices. "I'll have the death certificate ready for collection next week, if that's all right."

"We know she had … mental issues to deal with, but could that have been the cause?" Martha puzzled. "I mean—"

"It could have been a contributory factor, Mrs Booth," Dr Twist answered, a half-smile on his whiskered face as he fastened his coat and sidled towards the door. His pony and trap awaited him by the barn. "However, I believe she had come to a point where mentally she could no longer live without her husband, and so her body simply … gave up. We should search no further."

He stood for a short while by his horse, taking in the fresh air as he watched the light from the watery moon weave its way through the stately oak trees of ruinous age close by the dairy barn. He was getting to an age where he had witnessed more than enough deaths, and where he was beginning to feel that this latest of two within *this* family alone over the last few days was perhaps enough. Settling in the small carriage, he flicked the horse's rump with his deftly handled whip as an encouragement to set off. His mind wandered to a time when he would have no need to minister to the dead and dying.

"I think I'll have to stay here at least for tonight," George said to Poppy as the last guests took their leave. "There is no-one else to look after little Maisie, and she can't be left alone. Shall we—?"

"I won't be staying," Poppy stated unequivocally with little sign of emotion. "I have an early meeting with Peter Olleranshaw to publicise and promote my book. It's a meeting I cannot miss or postpone."

"But—?" George replied quickly, too stunned by her pronouncement to know what to say, as he watched her put on her coat. "Will you not stay at least *this* night?"

"I am afraid that I cannot and will not," she returned almost dismissively. "I have to prepare before I retire, and then tomorrow he will be arriving around eight in the morning."

As she could see where the present situation might be leading, she was starting to feel more than a little paranoid about having to shelve her lifetime's ambition to be a renowned and successful author – an ambition that was about to enjoy at least some degree of success.

"You never seem to come to bed at the same time as me these days," Poppy accused him sharply. "It seems usually to be towards early morning when most folk are getting ready to rise to their new day. I haven't really seen you for some days now. Have you found yourself another ... interest in your life?"

George sighed as he arose from his new uncomfortable

chair. He had heard all this before and didn't really want to enter into what had become a regular occurrence. As if he hadn't suffered enough with the recently traumatic burials within his family, let alone now having to bring up his one remaining child on his own.

"That *one* interest, as you only too well know, is my little daughter, Maisie," he reacted quite sharply. "She *has* to stay with us or there will be nowhere for her to go. If you don't want her with us, I will have to stay here with her – permanently – as this is the only home she has known."

"But you would still have the same problem in that you have to work," Poppy pointed out quite patiently. "We could hire a—"

"Nanny?" he scoffed dismissively. "Can't afford that, and anyway—"

"Sounds like the only solution to me, because I haven't the time," she re-joined quickly. "And—"

"Then *I* will look after her," a familiar voice butted in from the doorway.

Poppy turned sharply, recognising the voice immediately.

"Martha?" she uttered with a surprised gasp in her throat. "Why are you still here? Isn't it little Annie's bedtime by now?"

"Ross bathes and puts her to bed," she explained. "It's also their story time together. Sacrosanct. Well?"

"I can't let you do that!" George insisted. "You've your own nipper to look after, and ... what would Ross say?"

"Nothing to do with him," Martha scoffed. "Besides, your Maisie and our Annie are not that far apart in age. It'd do both good to have at least *one* friend."

"Not thinking of having any more of your own?" George asked, not sure what her response might be.

"*This* pregnancy was very hard, and Annie's birth almost finished me off," Martha explained quietly with a shudder. "I'm not sure I could go through that again."

"Can I not persuade you to stay … at least for a little while?" George persisted with Poppy, once he had settled his daughter to sleep in her own bed – without her twin sister.

"I can stay a little while and then I must away to Wisteria Cottage to prepare for tomorrow," Poppy explained, but added curtly. "By the way, will we be planning our … wedding any time soon?"

An uncomfortable silence inched its way into the room, leaving George no answer to give. He loved her with every inch of his being but so many things had intruded into his life to push the thoughts of marriage to the back of his mind. He had promised Poppy that once their new Scottish employee had settled in, their wedding plans would be put in place ready for the big day. He hadn't even *considered* all of this, much to Poppy's chagrin.

Without commenting further, Poppy arose and, seeking the door, disappeared into the darkness, on her way back to Wisteria Cottage and the solitude she often craved. Was life as George's wife going to be anything other than a mixture of broken promises and disappointments for her? She was beginning to fear the worst.

"Do you *ever* sleep?" Jenny Wilton asked as she let herself into the cottage at seven o'clock, to be greeted eagerly by Poppy bearing a tray of toasted brown bread, a monster China tea pot and two matching cups. "I didn't expect this!"

"Had very little to eat yesterday, what with one thing and another," Poppy returned with a giggle. "I find that sort of gathering incredibly draining. Toast and tea? Butter and marmalade?"

"You betcha!" Jenny drooled. "I've not had any breakfast either, and that looks divine!"

The log fire spluttered merrily in its grate, spitting the occasional spark alarmingly close to the clip rug that graced its stone hearth, and encouraged glorious warmth to circulate round their feet.

"Will Peter … Olleranshaw be joining us soon?" Poppy ventured, a slight pinkness suffusing her cheeks, almost in embarrassment. "Has he—?"

"At about eight o'clock, and … yes he has," Jenny interrupted. "He tells me that he read it at one lengthy sitting. Couldn't put it down. I have to say that **Faithfully Yours** captivated me, too. I think we have a monster there."

"Really?" Poppy responded with a gasp and a nervous giggle. "Is that—?"

"Both our opinions?" Jenny assured her. "Indeed, it is, undoubtedly."

A relaxed sigh escaped Poppy's lips as she polished off both tea and toast while delicately removing a smearing of marmalade from her mouth corners, much to the amusement of her friend. Poppy was excited to be seeing her publisher-to-be, as was the case when she had met him initially. A handsome man by any stretch of her imagination, who, no doubt, had captivated many a drooling wench previously.

"Looking forward to seeing Peter?" Jenny asked tentatively, drawing back her mind to Abigail's pointed comment about George the first time Peter Olleranshaw had appeared on Poppy's horizon.

"Indeed, I am," Poppy returned enthusiastically. "I bet he's a lady-killer, and no mistake."

"Actually, no, he's not," Jenny replied much to Poppy's surprise. "Never seems to have been too interested in having a partner. More interested in having his main reason for living, it seems … until now…"

"And that means?" Poppy puzzled, not really sure what she could be saying.

"Your book, your ability as a writer and … you," Jenny suggested, as a rattle on the door knocker echoed in the vestibule.

Chapter 6

"And how do you propose that we get ourselves to Nice?" Nell asked her husband rather sharply the first really foggy day this year in the depths of the North Riding. "Don't you think that we might need to make a move?"

"We can't use this magical new railway transport system because I don't think there's anything to take us from here to … there, yet." Ross replied with a heavy sigh. His breathing was becoming laboured and was causing him obvious difficulty. As usual with most things his needs had been shifted to the back of his mind because of more *urgent* happenings. "I'm waiting to hear back from a steamship company that offers regular passage from Southampton to Nice."

"Steamship company?" Nell returned apprehensively. "Wouldn't that be—?"

"Too expensive?" he butted in. "Money is no object, and, besides, I feel it has to be soon if I am to live out this winter."

"By soon, you mean?" Nell queried.

"Within the next couple of weeks," he suggested. "I have

arranged a suite in our usual hotel for two weeks today. So, you'd better start packing."

"But what about—?" she replied with a deep sigh of resignation.

"Our house and belongings in Richmond?" he said. "I've already had a word with our Ross to move on that one. He had the same reservations as you seem to have but has agreed to set things in motion. I'm expecting to receive a reply from my contact within the next day or two."

"And if you don't?" she asked. "I—"

She was interrupted by an urgent banging on their front door, prompting Ross to disappear into the hallway.

Things were moving too quickly for Nell, who had thought they would have many years where they were, sharing the future with their immediate family, watching proudly their grandchildren grow in stature. They hoped also for great-grandchildren, too, perhaps, to follow in their footsteps. Now time seemed to be becoming shorter and more urgent. Would she be able to enjoy their retirement together for much longer?

"And?" she hissed as he came back into their living room. "What is that paper you are wafting at me?"

"The response I have been waiting for from the steamship company," he explained with a relieved grin as he plumped his backside into the settee. "We sail from Southampton in five days. We need to start our packing today."

"Today?" she retorted with almost a disdainful snort. "It's almost finished. I've been putting stuff into t'owd trunk you brought from Australia for nigh on two months now. Do you know what the best part of that is? You neither missed your things nor did you know."

He shuffled across the settee, put his arm around her shoulders and drew her unresisting body to his. His love for her knew no bounds as they looked into each other's eyes and with a nod arose to finish this packing.

"I'll speak to Ross this evening," Ross Senior suggested. "Over dinner at the Royal, perhaps?"

"I'd ask the three of them – Ross, Martha and little Annie – over here tomorrow, and then we can discuss matters in private," she said. "Five days, eh? Can't wait. Oh for the warmth of the South of France at last!"

"Does this mean that this will be the last we'll see of you?" Ross asked of his mother, a concerned look playing around his face.

"Apart from your coming over to stay with us in our new home – when we have it," she explained. "You will be able to bring little Annie, won't you?"

"Can't see it, realistically, Mother," Ross answered with a shrug. "We're having serious issues with costing for all produce in most areas, even though we are working flat out most of the time."

"How come?" Ross Senior asked, knowing full well that his usual suggestion of throwing money at the problem would not be the answer during the present down-turn.

"The markets just aren't there as they used to be," his son explained. "We are almost having to give away produce to ensure some sort of a turnover. We *need* things to pick up because we can't *make* them."

Silence descended while pudding was consumed slowly, and worries built.

"Anyway, we'll get you two off to your nirvana first to make sure Father's health gets no worse, and then we'll see how things are," Ross offered.

"Perhaps this is as good a time as any to announce that we are expecting our second child," Martha dropped leisurely into the conversation.

Nell's face said it all. Knocking over her chair as she rushed to hug her daughter-in-law, she couldn't contain her delight that Granddaughter Little Annie, was about to have a brother or sister to grow up with.

"How are things with George's little'un, Maisie?" Nell asked carefully. "We know there have been … difficulties."

"Maisie *is* finding life a challenge without her twin to lean on but seems to be developing a welcome relationship with our Annie," Martha revealed. "Only time will tell. Slow progress when only improvements can be made. George is finding life difficult at the moment, what with the loss of his other daughter and his mother."

"How are you finding his relationship with Poppy?" Ross Senior asked.

"Not my – our – place to comment," Martha responded with a non-committal grimace. "You'll have to ask them about that one, I'm afraid."

Nell's look towards her husband said it all, surprised at his unusual lack of finesse and feeling. They both knew that things weren't right with them, particularly with George's attitude towards planning for their marriage. Nell sympathised with her granddaughter's impatience at his ineptitude and lack of urgency. Although not sleeping together, she, at least, had committed herself to him mentally in the hope that they would be together legally, mentally and spiritually as soon as possible. Nell, however, wasn't sure about Poppy's attitude towards having children. *Her* all-consuming passion had been, was and would always be writing for as long as her nanny could foresee. Poppy's insistence on marriage before sex was unequivocal and unchangeable, and this George had accepted. So why hadn't he committed physically?

This was a question Poppy didn't understand and wouldn't relent upon, certainly for the foreseeable future. Was George serious in his stated intention to marry her? If so, why hadn't he done so already? Could it be his way of cooling things down between them?

CHAPTER 7

"I still can't get my head around what Peter Olleranshaw has offered," Poppy uttered quietly incredulous over what he had to say about her story. "Publish and launch within two months?"

"You'd better believe it, Miss Poppy Spence!" Jenny Wilton reassured her friend. "He is very serious about ***Faithfully Yours***. He has suggested only one or two very minor alterations that you can leave to him to attend to. Then it should take off like the proverbial bat out of hell."

"But how do I get people to read it, bearing in mind where we live, and the rest of the country is a million miles away?" Poppy queried, a look of apprehensive shock in her eyes.

"You don't," Jenny said. "Your publisher will see to all that, including the launch and distribution of all available copies. Bear in mind also that as books become more available to a wider audience, more educated people will be wanting to acquire a copy of *your* wonderful stories."

"And in the meantime?" Poppy asked, still unsure of which way to go.

"Enjoy the excitement and joy that you have come so far over the last few years," her friend advised. "Perhaps also thinking about a … sequel?"

"Following on from Peter's advice, I have already started it," Poppy replied with a smile. "Once this one has been launched, **And Now?** will be on its way big style."

"Heavens above!" Jenny gasped. "Don't hold back, will you!"

They both laughed, happy that Poppy was beginning to immerse herself into this new life that becoming an author was offering her. She often wondered to herself how Florence would have handled all of this … unreality. She would probably have taken it all in her stride. But would she?

Family life and pregnancy had dealt her a wicked blow by removing all of her aspirations to become what Poppy was beginning to experience. *She*, however, was letting nothing either stand in her way or divert her from her chosen path. She *would* succeed without a doubt. She would see to that.

But what about George? And what would she do about Peter should he approach her? She felt that George had more important things on his mind that didn't involve planning for their impending nuptials, and she was convinced that he knew she wouldn't put up with it. How wrong was he! She was patient – to a point – but beyond that point she could walk away. The question was how far away was that point, and how quickly would she put herself first?

"Penny?" Jenny asked quietly.

"How do you mean?" Poppy returned, emerging quickly from her reverie, not quite understanding what her friend was saying. "And would you stop calling me 'Penny'?"

"Penny for your thoughts," Jenny explained with a giggle. "It's a saying. You seemed to have been far away for the last ten minutes or so, and it's a way of drawing you back into the here and now."

"I was thinking through my future moves," Poppy answered vaguely.

"Between George and … Peter?" Jenny asked intuitively.

"My, you are so deep, my dear friend!" Poppy challenged. "Was it that obvious?"

"Well, they have become the two most likely difficulties you are struggling with – marry George or become interested in Peter," Jenny explained. "Seems obvious to me. Doesn't it?"

"Between you and me," Poppy offered, "George seems to be procrastinating seriously about our agreement to consider our wedding as a matter of urgency. I know he has been beset with sadness enough to try anyone's resolve, but setting our day should be a logical healer, shouldn't it?"

"I should have thought so – if he *is* serious," Jenny said. "Do you think he's serious?"

"I thought so, at one stage," Poppy responded. "But now I'm not so sure. It's almost as if I'm not here – invisible on the side-lines."

"Time for an ultimatum, perhaps?" her friend suggested. "After all, he wasn't *so* slow to wed Florence … or Alice for that matter."

"You're right!" Poppy agreed, a stern light of resolve starting to burn in her eyes.

"Your call, my dear friend, but I believe you deserve to know," Jenny added. "After all, he was the one to come to *you*."

<hr>

"No, I haven't been able to resolve totally our employee problem yet, my dearest Poppy," George replied to her sharp question once again about their future over tea at Wisteria

Cottage. "And I must be off very soon to collect Maisie from Martha's."

"Then, don't come back here," she retorted pointedly. "If you are not even prepared to discuss our future, there is no point in our being together. I feel that you have been stringing me along with no desire to be married to me at all!"

Tears sprang to her eyes as she steeled herself against his probable response, only to have her resolve hardened by his angry outburst against her.

"Then we might as well call off any *thoughts* of weddings," he snarled, leaping to his feet and storming out of the room.

She heard the loud snap of the outside door's latch as he left. George was obviously no longer *her* George, as his response to her outburst was not what she had wanted or expected.

"Poppy! Poppy!" Ross's voice echoed from the front door vestibule. "You in?"

"Uncle Ross!" Poppy called back as he joined her. "If you're looking for George, he has just set off for yours, and—"

"Any reason why he was in some sort of a mood?" he asked.

"Mood?" she replied. "How do you mean?"

"Walked in through our front door, and without a word, he picked up his daughter and headed out towards their farm," Ross explained. "Is anything wrong?"

She beckoned him to come sit with her while she cleared the tears from her eyes and explained what had just happened.

"That can't be the reason, surely, can it?" he puzzled.

"He has not once committed to becoming my husband, Uncle Ross," she went on tremulously. "I've asked and asked for us to set a date when we could walk down the aisle together as husband and wife, and it's always been put off because of issue or another to do with running the farm. Everything came to a head over tea."

"I know things have been busy but problems to a large extent have been alleviated by our newish staff appointments and—" he went on.

"Newish staff appointments?" she queried quickly. "But I thought that that's where the problems lay?"

"Been sorted for some time really, with things moving on quite smoothly," he said with a guarded look.

"Then there's the reason why we aren't getting married!" she responded sharply. "I won't accept any more excuses!"

"I don't understand," he said, tipping his head and raising an eyebrow quizzically.

"His excuse has always been pressure of work and lack of staff, reiterated only this evening over tea," she explained. "I don't expect to see him again because I too have a busy time ahead."

"*Faithfully Yours?*" he responded with a knowing grin. "Can't wait to read it."

She explained how busy she thought she was going to be as she walked her uncle to the door and out onto the driveway.

"The first dedicated copy will be yours, Uncle Ross!" she called as he made his crunchy way back to the Big House.

He waved as he reached its porticoes before disappearing inside.

"Everything all right, my husband?" Martha asked.

"I'm afraid not," he started to explain, a saddened look growing in his stubbly face, as he told her what had come to pass.

"George has always been headstrong for as long as I can remember, and more than a little disorganised," Martha reacted. "The problem that inevitably comes with being a young boy in a house full of older females. Dad never had much of a say in how the household was either organised or run. That doesn't excuse for a minute how he has been treating dear Poppy. Possibly not something suited to her – being a farmer's wife, I mean."

"She needs to be free to do whatever satisfies her," Ross agreed. "Writing is a passion she needs to be able to pursue and develop. That doesn't involve the clever way a good farmer's wife organises and runs *her* domain. It seems like the passion that has been growing since she was an eleven-year-old is now coming to maturity and fruition getting on for two decades later."

"I'm looking forward to reading the finished product," his wife said, rubbing her hands together in anticipation. "***Faithfully Yours***, isn't it?"

"It's a great shame, though," Ross acknowledged. "They seem to have had such feelings for one another."

"Not enough, Ross," she returned. "You for example, my man, always thought deeply about me and my welfare throughout, and that is the only way a relationship can deepen and last forever."

"I love you very much, too, my little sparrow," he said quietly, drawing his wife to him. "I—"

"Mammy! Daddy!" a pleading little voice swept over them from the head of the stairs. "Not can sleep. Story, please Daddy?"

"All right my little one," Ross called as he leaped to his feet, mounting the stairs to his little Annie to settle her down. He picked her up and threw her into the air to her squeals of delight. "There was once a little princess…"

Martha smiled at how this man could settle their little one in an instant and make her happy at the same time. That's how a husband and father should be. Everything to the whole family.

George sat in the dark of his daughter's bedroom, staring out through the window into the pitch-black night. What had just happened? Why had he lied to his Poppy about the situation in the farm? Why couldn't he have done everything he had promised her about their future together to support his feelings for her? Now what? Would it be possible to undo the wrongs he had wrought in their relationship? Perhaps not, but what should he do to alleviate the unhappiness he had subjected her to?

What a selfish bugger he had become! Had the death of two wives, a beloved infant, and his mother brought him to this?

No excuses! No shifting his wrong doings!

The blame lay squarely on his more than ample shoulders.

CHAPTER 8

"Abigail! Hal!" Poppy called gleefully as she caught sight of a pony and trap crunching noisily up the driveway with two very recognisable people occupying its front seat, with a small person lodged between them. "It seems like I've not seen you for an eon. How are you all, and how is little Grace?"

"I am very well, thank you Aunt Poppy," the scrap of humanity sitting between her mother and father piped up. "How be you?"

Abigail leaned over to whisper in her daughter's ear.

"How *are* you?" Grace corrected herself.

"It's lovely to see you, Grace," Poppy answered, with a huge grin. "And I thank you for your good wishes. Come in. Come in. Afternoon tea will be ready in a short while, prepared by Mary-Jane who will be eating with us."

"Looking forward to that if it's as good as the food we got when I proposed to my wonderful lady at Mary's Pantry!" Hal said enthusiastically, drooling mentally at the thought.

"We have already been in contact with our relatives in Paris and Rome to publicise your book, and they, along with *their* very wide circle of family and friends, are very avid readers," Abigail alerted Poppy. "You will have a very large following there. Word will also spread among the expatriate populations hugely."

"I can't believe what you are doing for me," Poppy gasped almost at the point of tears.

"It's what we do, particularly for you, dear Poppy," Hal added with a nod and smile. "You *are* special, don't forget."

"Hal has also arranged for a variety of events around the official launch – one in London, one in Paris – not sure about Rome yet," Abigail said. "We'll manage those with you and accompany you to them all."

"That's wonderful!" Poppy rejoiced. "Have you been doing anything else exciting since last we met?"

"Hal was exploring possibilities in London when Queen Victoria died," Abigail added, "but I'll leave that to Hal to tell you about that experience."

"Six thirty pm on Tuesday 22nd January 1901," he started, "at Osborne House. She was eighty-one years old. She is said to have died from a cerebral haemorrhage. As she died on the Isle of Wight, her body was carried on board Her Majesty's Yacht Alberta, with several yachts carrying mourners, including her eldest son and new monarch, Edward VII, to Gosport in Hampshire. It was then taken by train to Victoria Station in London."

"My word!" Poppy gasped. "How do you know all that?"

"You know my Hal," Abigail returned "It's what he does."

"And *I* know that, before she was put in her coffin," little Grace butted in, "she was dressed in white."

"That's ma girl!" Hal added with a grin.

"Her father's daughter," Abigail sighed.

"Not to forget the Queen's wedding veil and mementos

such as her husband's dressing gown and a plaster cast of his hand were placed in her coffin with her," Hal finished.

"I suppose a lot of businesses would have closed down on the day?" Poppy questioned.

"Indeed, yes," Hal agreed. "There was also a full military service, with her coffin carried on a gun carriage pulled by white horses. Strangely, though, there was no lying in state. She was Queen for sixty-three years and seven months from 1837, don't forget."

"Very interesting," Abigail added. "If you value that sort of thing."

"She had always decreed," Hal carried on unabashed, "that her funeral should be a white affair. On the evening of 4th February, her coffin was taken to Frogmore Mausoleum, Windsor, that she had had built for Albert upon *his* death. Interestingly, above the mausoleum's doors, she had had inscribed:

Vale desideratissime. Farewell most beloved.
Here at length, I shall rest with thee,
and with thee in Christ I shall rise again.

Almost all commercial activity in the country ground to a halt. Theatre stuff was put on hold and businesses closed and prepared to buy black mourning clothes. I say, Mary-Jane, this afternoon tea looks, smells and tastes delicious."

"Ever the practical chap, eh Hal!" Abigail laughed, not expecting an answer because of his full mouth.

Mary-Jane smiled that her efforts had proved to be success-ful. She had learned a lot from her Aunt Mary, despite her poor start at home with her mother. Father left when she was a tiny four-year-old, and she never saw him again. Mother never had any money, and it was only because her sister, Mary, stepped in to help that Mary-Jane was able to develop her skills in her chosen occupation, becoming a first-class cook, baker and food caterer.

"I never knew anything about this except for the time Mary-Jane came to Boulders Wood to be taught by Mary, our cook, just about time she decided to do business with the shop in Richmond that was destined to become **Mary's Pantry**," Poppy said. "I can remember the mince pies and Christmas cakes and pasties she used to make. They were delicious right from the off – and are so today."

"Don't know why, but cooking and baking are things I have always wanted to do," Mary-Jane explained. "As Mother had no income since my father left – never had any while he was there either – I felt I had to earn so we could live."

"Did your father *ever* return?" Abigail asked, upset by what she was hearing.

"Never did," Mary-Jane replied with a sneer. "He was an unpleasant individual. I remember once when he made a 'move' on me, she saw what he was trying to do and hit him across the back of the head with a frying pan she happened to have in her hand. Knocked him out cold. It wasn't long after that he disappeared."

"Don't you live in Richmond now?" Abigail asked.

"Indeed, I do," she responded vigorously. "My mam lives with me, too, in my flat. She's not very well at the moment, but we manage."

"If there's anything we can do to help…?" Abigail added.

"It's all right … really," Mary-Jane responded with a grateful smile. "We are managing, what with my work at Boulders Wood and the occasional stint with my Aunt Mary, plus one or two other private events."

"The world is lucky to have such a lovely lady as you, Mary-Jane," Hal interjected. "However, seriously, if there is ever any way we can be of assistance – we have significant contacts that could be useful to you – please don't hesitate to let us know. If, for example, you might want to set up your own business similar to that one your aunt has set up…?"

"Thank you for your kindness," she responded gratefully. "I will, but at the moment I have only twenty-four hours in my day, and I need also to look after my mother. Also, I wouldn't like to be in competition with Aunt Mary because—"

"We understand, but the offer will always be there," he added with a nod.

"Actually, your Aunt Mary has a very high regard for your attributes and abilities," Poppy butted in. "I know, too, that she feels so overwhelmed at **Mary's Pantry** on many occasions that she has said might like to expand and have someone – like you – take over more."

"Really?" Mary-Jane said with a genuine look of surprise in her face. "I would love that. Anyway, it's been lovely talking with you and preparing our afternoon tea. I—"

"Leave the pots and crockery to us," Abigail insisted, allowing her to slip her coat around her shoulders in readiness for her walk into the village to seek a taxi.

"Oh, by the way," Hal interrupted. "How are you considering getting home? It looks a bit like rain. Don't answer that one. I have arranged for a cab to pick you up here round about … now. So, if you would like to hang on a few moments…"

"But I can't—!" she responded quickly.

"Oh, yes you can!" Abigail and Poppy chorused. "We can hear him now."

"It's the least we can do, my dear," Hal's voice joined in.

"Your safety means the world to us. We have known the cab driver for many years. I'll see you out."

"A lovely young lady," Hal said once he had regained the cottage's warmer interior. "We must keep an eye on her well-being, both professionally and personally. Her mother seems to be exhibiting similar traits to those carried by George's mother, perhaps?"

"It's a possibility," Poppy replied. "But don't forget that Mary has her interests at heart, too. After all, she is her blood niece. Mary isn't likely to let her languish through lack of support. She is the one that saw her potential when she – Mary – was about to spread *her* wings into *her* business world. Perhaps I might mention to Mary—?"

"I should leave that one to Hal," Abigail suggested. "He is perhaps the best person to broach the subject. He is very good at that sort of thing."

"Can I assume you will be staying over tonight?" Poppy suggested. "The two bedrooms are ready which includes the special bedroom for someone called … Grace."

"Grace?" Abigail said, turning towards her daughter. "Would you like to stay here tonight with Auntie Poppy?"

"*I* will … if *you* will," Grace responded after a moment or two's thought. "I do like it here because it's quiet and I like to see all the birds and skirwills in trees and—"

"*Squirrels,* my sweetheart," Abigail corrected gently. "So, it's decided then. We would love to stay. Having said that, I think it's getting towards Haltime. Don't you, my darling?"

"Yes, Mamma," Grace agreed. "Baff and story and bedtime."

"Hal?" Abigail went on.

"Indeed," Hal added, turning towards his delightful daughter. "Cherub?"

"Coming, Daddy," Grace replied as she sprang from the settee by the fire. "When *you* are ready."

They trooped off to the bathroom, ready to spend the next hour together preparing for bedtime.

"They love to spend this time together," Abigail explained once husband had left the room with daughter sitting in his arms. "He adores his beautiful little diamond that only he could have made. She is like him in so many ways."

Crepuscular evening began to warn of its approach as Poppy drew the curtains and made to stoke the ever-shrinking flames in the fire grate. This time was usually her most productive period in each day, with most of her serious ideas for developing actions as they flowed into her erudite and creative lines and scenes. Today, however, she needed not to immerse herself in fiction, but to enjoy the company of her dearest friends to try to make sense of the recent happenings in her *real* private life.

"How are things with George these days?" Abigail asked. "Any closer to closure over marriage?"

"It's all off, I'm afraid," Poppy said dropping almost to a saddening whisper.

"Off? Where to?" her friend said, almost too frightened to ask her to explain. "Anywhere nice?"

"Off in that we will *not* be getting married," Poppy added, continuing to explain recent events. "He has procrastinated setting the date for such a long time that I am convinced it is not important to him. He would have us living together – unmarried – as did his parents, never bothering to legalise our relationship, whereas—"

"You wouldn't?" her friend interrupted. "Good for you! Fortunately, I didn't need to push my Hal. He feels much the same as you, and rightly so. Stick to your guns, girl!"

"There will be no need because I have called off our association and brought our relationship to its – unhappy – end," Poppy said, finally sure of where she wanted to be.

"Next moves?" Abigail asked tentatively.

"One hundred per cent with moving forward with my passion for storytelling," she explained. "These characters are my true brothers, sisters and … lovers, and I will not let them down, whatever the situation in *my* life. I am very much looking forward to introducing them to a wider audience through you and Hal, wherever that may take us. Wake up, New World! We are coming for you!"

George's mind had hit a brick wall following his unexpected split from Poppy. How could he have let *that* happen? He knew full well how and why. How could he not know after his angry walk out from the home he had come to like and feel comfortable in? His inactivity and lack of thought about what was important to her had let *him* down and, more importantly, his Poppy. All he had had to do was sit down with her to set a wedding date that was acceptable to her, but he was so self-obsessed, he couldn't even do that.

So, what now? Would he be able to win her back? Knowing her views and feelings concerning loyalty and truthfulness, he thought it would perhaps be unlikely.

Now here he was, in the depths of depression, the love of his life disappearing into anonymity before his eyes.

He didn't know whether he could accept that, or even live without the love that had sustained him throughout all his troubles for such a long time.

He arose from his chair sharply to see to his daughter's cry, came over dizzy and collapsed to the floor unconscious.

CHAPTER 9

"And I can't see how we are going to cope with things as they are," Joseph said to his brother over their customary very early breakfast before the start of their usually busy day.

"It's a phase, Brother," Ross reacted through a mouthful of his double-yolked egg and bacon. "We've been here before and we've survived even stronger."

"The Tythe Land Agents are like leeches that are grabbing more of our returns as time goes on," Joseph pointed out. "They seem to be wanting us to fail."

"They've no chance of that," Ross assured him. "There are ways of circumventing what the Tythe Act of 1890 insists that we pay."

"Legal ways, I hope," his brother urged.

"Never any other way, I can promise you," Ross replied, ever sure of himself.

"How can that be?" Joseph asked, puzzled how his brother could have worked that one out.

"There are ways of off-setting what we are losing in sales against what we are having to pay in taxes," Ross explained carefully. "Our most pressing issue is what we have to do about George."

"George?" his brother said, nonplussed as to what he might mean. "Why? What's the problem with George? He's had no further issues with Jonas Jamieson, has he?"

"Keep up, Brother! Keep up," Ross smiled. "He and Poppy are no more."

"When? Why did that happen?" Joseph said with a shrug of his ample shoulders and a slight shake of the head.

"You above all else should be able to empathise with that one," Ross tried to explain.

Still not able to relate, Ross reminded him of the problems he and Lilly Victoria had in their early days of having children.

"It all comes down to overwork and blinkered vision," Ross reminded him, to his brother's blank look, shake of the head and spreading his arms in non-understanding.

"Surely you've not forgotten when Lilly Victoria left with your children and went to stay with her parents because you were working too long and too hard every day?" Ross reminded him. "It was also a case of not employing enough folks to take some of the burden off your shoulders. Remember?"

"Ouch!" his brother replied with a wince. "I do now!"

"Same thing with George, only he's been promising to employ, *and* plan their wedding for some time," Ross added. "He employed the Scot, Hamish, some time ago, but reneged on the second part of the deal. Apparently, he stormed out of the cottage in a temper, and they've been apart ever since. All attention now is on the launch."

"Launch?" Joseph puzzled, as if not living in the same world as everyone else in the family.

"Her book? *Faithfully Yours*?" Ross uttered quietly trying to remind him gently. "Remember? Apparently, according to Cousin Hal, it's going to be a cracker."

"How on earth could he know whether folks outside this little area are going to want to read?" Joseph sneered naively.

"Are you *trying* to be a dodo, Bro, or is it natural?" Ross sniggered. "Drag yourself into our modern world! Hal and Abigail have travelled the length and breadth of Europe publicising the launch, with a significant amount of interest in this new female author."

"And who is *she* when she's at home?" his brother scoffed.

"Oh, just somebody called … Poppy Spence, who is, in fact, your … blood niece," Ross guffawed, aghast at his insular ignorance. "Our POPPY!!"

Joseph closed his mouth in clear embarrassment, now aware of how much he didn't know about his own family.

"The real world beckons, O Brother!" Ross advised. "George has made almost the same mistakes as you did, but this time he will have a much higher price to pay."

⁓

"Peter Olleranshaw! Fancy meeting you here!" Poppy gasped, virtually bumping into the publisher as she made her way into Mary's Pantry for afternoon tea.

"I have been going to ask you out for some time, but you have been very busy of late, and so have I," he returned as he held the door open for her to enter. As they did, Mary ushered them to a table for two in the bay window which overlooked the busy thoroughfare beyond its blemish-free transparent screen before it.

"I didn't know you frequented this wonderful emporium," he went on as they sat down.

"I have known Mary here for more years than I can recall," Poppy explained. "She's more like family to me who has always been there for me since I was a little girl."

"Then, this occasion has to be my treat," he declared, looking steadfastly into her eyes. Mary, of course, knew what Poppy's order would be and so had decided that this new man should enjoy the same.

"Are you ready for your new adventure?" he asked her, not really knowing what her response might be, thinking perhaps that it all might be overwhelming for her. "One launch locally?"

"Actually, no," she began to explain in detail about her mini launch the coming Friday among her colleagues and friends at her literary group meeting at Wisteria Cottage. "Everything else then takes off in stages from Blueberry's Bookshop in Richmond to Pritchard's in London within a week, to be followed shortly after by Paris and perhaps Rome."

"How on earth have you managed to organise all of that?" he gasped, having to replace cup to saucer quickly so as not to spill. "That—"

"Has been arranged by my agents, who will also be accompanying me on all my travels," Poppy giggled slightly, seeing the look of shocked surprise imprinted on his face.

"That's amazing," he commented in admiration. "Who are these magical mystery maestros?"

"They are Abigail and Hal McIntyre who are good and very clever friends," Poppy announced with pride. "She used to be one of the Times Newspaper's best reporters, and he is the most amazing explorer, adventurer and diamond miner in the whole world. I am very fortunate to count them as close friends and associates. We are all looking forward to the next few months with excitement, which will, hopefully, publicise my story writing in a very positive fashion."

"Then this will be the best published book ever," Peter agreed. "I have to say, too, that I enjoyed its reading enormously, and can't wait for its sequel."

"A follow-on to this story?" she said with a degree of surprise.

"Indeed. It's a must that has to follow pretty quickly on the heels of one's success. Your audience will demand it, and you cannot, must not, let them down," he assured her.

This man was becoming more attractive by the minute!

However, was it because of his positively complimentary comments about her writing? Or was there something else?

"Auntie Charity! Auntie Charity!" George's daughter, Maisie, urged her sleeping aunt to consciousness as she lay soundly asleep in the bed once occupied by Tom and Lilly Garside, Maisie's grandparents.

"Maisie?" Charity asked as she sat up in bed, concerned why her niece was *here* waking *her*. "What is it?"

"Quick!" Maisie urged. "Daddy's on the floor asleep and I can't wake him. I need the toilet."

Charity drew on her dressing gown as she hurried to find out what was the matter with her brother.

"My God! George?" Charity gasped as she tried to wake him. A slight oozing of blood from his right ear made her realise that this was not meant to be, as he groaned, opened his eyes slowly and tried to sit up.

"Steady," she advised as she dressed and cleaned the wound, led him towards his bed, and settled him before taking his daughter to perform her ablutions.

"Is Daddy all right?" Maisie asked in a whisper so as not to wake him again. "Is he going to … die like Nanna and my Alice?"

"No, my lovely," Charity replied as she settled the child into her bed. "He's just a bit … tired. He works very hard, you know. Now, back to sleep, eh? He'll be all right in the morning."

"Promise?" the child asked desperately. She had suffered so much trauma over the last months that she didn't know what to believe.

"Promise. Now back off to sleep," Charity urged. "You'll see in the morning."

Charity slept fitfully for the rest of the night, not understanding why her brother had entered a state of mind she had never seen before. Was it to do with everything that had happened to him lately, including the loss of his two wives, one five-year-old child, and his mother? It had taken him some time to come to terms with his father's passing, but now…

She knew nothing about George's altercation with Poppy other than he had not seen her for a day or two, and that she put down to pressure of work. She hadn't spoken to him much either, but when George was up to his eyeballs in toil, he rarely spoke to anyone. Always had been a loner ever since childhood; it's what having four older sisters did for you! Not a spoiled child by any stretch of the imagination. The only friends he ever had were Florence and Poppy, and those relationships were hit and miss a lot of the times.

She stole quietly into his room at about the time he usually got up, to find that his bed had been slept *on* but not *in*. The clothes he had worn the day before were not there – perhaps he had them on again for work, or perhaps he was at Wisteria Cottage with Poppy.

When Poppy called to collect Maisie to take her to spend the day with Martha and her little daughter, Annie, Charity realised that he couldn't have been with Poppy. At that point alarm bells started ringing. Maisie wasn't in *her* room either.

"Now here's the problem," Charity said, quite disturbed at what she didn't understand, starting to tell Poppy about the difficulties she had with George in the early hours of the morning. "He's not here, but neither is Maisie."

When Poppy gave her the gist of his behaviour towards her, and at Ross and Martha's, Charity began to panic about their whereabouts at this time of day.

"I'll go back and check to see if he has dropped her off at Boulders Wood, and then I'll let *you* know," Poppy said, not too concerned about George, but more than a little worried about his daughter's whereabouts."

"Not here, I'm afraid, Poppy," Ross told her, also concerned. "I've not seen him anywhere around the farm, and I've been up for more than a couple of hours. I've no idea where we could look, unless he's taken her with him on his rounds, and that would be a non-starter, I can assure you."

"Do you think I could—?" Poppy started, to be interrupted sternly by her uncle.

"Certainly not!" he rebutted, knowing full well what her suggestion might be. "We have no way of knowing his round. There are so many ways he could deliver his goods, and only he knows where and how. You could be travelling round in circles for a week and still not find him."

"*Then* what?" she insisted.

"We'll have to wait until he turns up wherever-whenever," Ross said as he left the house for the fields and his business with Jim Smallshore.

Poppy set off back to Garside Farm not knowing how to break the news about George and his daughter's whereabouts, feeling that they may have a major tragedy on their hands.

Chapter 10

"As far as I am concerned, Toby, my lad, you are my son and will always be treated as such," Jonas said to the lad early one morning, "No matter whether your mother agrees to marry me, or not."

"But—" Toby butted in, not really knowing what to say.

"Of course, if you don't want it to be so, all you have to do is to say 'No'," Jonas interrupted, causing the lad to frown and to shake his head slowly.

"That's not the point, Mr Jamieson," the lad urged. "I would love for that to have been so, but obviously I am not your son, because I was born before my mother met you. I believe she knows who my real father is, and so my real family is out there … somewhere. If you marry my mother, I believe you would become my stepfather, and that is fine, but I would still like to find him, wherever *he* is."

Jonas fell quiet, not expecting such a reasoned and honest response from the lad. His mother had had so many partners that his father could have been anyone, and there would be no real way of tracking him down. Perhaps it might have been polite to accept Jonas Jamieson's offer and to *belong* like never before. But he had decided he needed an opportunity at least to try.

"Would that be all right for you?" Toby asked. "However, I do need my mother to agree to your request for me to even consider our relationship further."

"You will have to pursue whatever avenues suit you, Old Chap," Jonas agreed. "You will probably find that it's a thankless task, but I'm going nowhere, and my offer will always stand however fruitless your research might prove to become. If your mother accepts the offer from this unworthy one and a half-legged beggar, then at least one link will be forged for you."

He reached for his crutches to help him to hobble to their wonderfully new jakes with its fabulous flushing system designed by Thomas Crapper himself, a contraption that would always hold a large degree of wonder for him. His experiences over many fruitless years held deep roots in his subconscious that he could never visit these new-fangled wonders too many times, and he had no visions of ever returning to those other dire bygone days.

"Mother?" Toby said to Jenny in their new palatial kitchen.

"Yes, my son, what can I get you?" she replied.

"Do you have any idea who my father might be?" he asked after explaining what Jonas had said to him.

She sat down on one of their new chairs with a resigned bump, about to explain their situation as far as she was able.

"Two possibilities, I suppose, one of whom is undoubtedly now dead," she started.

"A local farmer, maybe?" he added much to her surprise. "And the other?"

"How did you work that one out?" she said trying to hide in her surprise.

"Never mind, and the other?" he persisted eagerly.

"You have no chance of pursuing that line because you won't get anywhere with it," she explained slowly. "I have no proof of that or of his paternity. He is so wealthy we would have no chance of proving any claim we think we might want to pursue."

"That person might be?" Toby persisted, hoping he might be able to shed light on her past associations.

"I can neither remember nor would I wish to try," she remarked. "If you were to insist, the strong likelihood might be that you would take over the flea pit of a dungeon that Jonas relinquished by the skin of his teeth. Let it drop. End of conversation."

The lad fell silent, loth to let go of his one opportunity to discover his sire, not understanding that even if his mother could remember one distinct liaison that might have proved to be fruitful, there was no way it could have been proved to be the case. The word of a known harlot would never have been accepted.

"By the way," she continued after a moment of hissing silence. "I have decided to wed Jonas Jamieson, giving him the opportunity to settle and look after us. I assume you have the sense to accept this God-given chance to live an acceptable life where we can afford the niceties such a life will bring?"

"I know," he agreed. "It's just—"

"Yet, I am convinced he will make an excellent stepfather," Jenny added, "affording you opportunities to develop and follow your own path to whatever success you might aspire."

Jonas hobbled back into the kitchen from the bathroom on his crutches.

"Does anyone fancy a spot of lunch?" he asked as he shuffled his backside into an easy chair by the garden window.

"Yes, indeed," she agreed. "In a while. Just one thing to discuss before that."

"And that is?" he returned, unsure of where she was leading him.

"My answer, too, is 'yes'," she responded.

"Has this house suddenly become inhabited by 'yes' people?" Jonas smiled benignly, still not sure where this conversation was leading.

"Yes, I *will* marry you, Jonas Jamieson," she blurted out, knocking him back into his chair, still not quite sure what he was hearing.

He remained in his seat, shocked into stunned silence, not expecting *that* answer any time soon.

"It's time we built our life that most *ordinary* people would consider acceptable, and the sooner the better," she went on. "Any dates in mind? A week on Thursday, for example?"

A look of excited joy leaped into his face as his eyes flicked from mother to son.

"And you, Young Toby?" he said.

"*I'm* not going to marry you!" the lad said with a guffaw. "I would be delighted to become your stepson, if that's acceptable?"

～

"Are you sure this is what you really want to do?" Ross asked his mother and father at York Railway Station as they waited for the early morning train to take them to London on the first leg of their journey to the South of France.

"No," Ross Senior retorted. "It is certainly not how we envisaged the course of our life might run. Periodic holidays there, yes, but not escaping our beloved home and family to try to alleviate an insidious illness that will take me out if we don't do as we are doing. Little did I know when I emigrated to Australia because I wasn't able to be with the woman I loved and would have to escape again in later life."

"We will, of course, want to come visit once our new little scallywag is with us," Ross Junior assured them. "That may be some time away, though. It also depends on what I can find out about the railways across France."

"Across France?" Nell asked, not sure what he was saying.

"We don't want to sail to Nice as you are doing," Martha explained. "Trains seem to be an excellent idea, but for me anything to do with water is a no, I'm afraid."

"Of course," Ross Senior agreed. "We will look into that one when we are settled. You must be aware also that we have gifted our house in Richmond to Poppy on the understanding that should she sell it when she makes it big-time because of her writing, the proceeds must be split three ways."

"As in…?" Martha puzzled.

"A third each to you two, Joseph and his bunch, and, of course, to Poppy," Ross Senior explained. "It's been settled with our solicitor. The reason being that we shall not return, ever. My specialist has warned me that a return to this harsh fog-laden atmosphere at any time could prove to be fatal. Consequently, our *permanent* home will be on the Cote d'Azur."

"The train will be here soon, so we would like you to bid us farewell *now*, and not stand around waving our carriage 'goodbye' as it disappears and we all become upset at its passing," Nell added. "We hope to see you in the not-too-distant future."

"That's our train now," Ross Senior added, as a shrill hooting sound interrupted their conversation. "So, we'll bid our farewells here."

"Mammy?" little Annie's pert voice piped in. "Why are we leaving Nanny and Grandpa here?"

"They are going away on holiday to somewhere the sun always shines, my sweetheart," Martha replied. "It's too cold here for them to stay. We'll see them again a little later on when it gets a bit warmer."

"May we have an ice cream, Daddy, please?" she piped up again.

"Of course we may," he reacted with a smile. "Let's leave the railway station and see what we can find, eh?"

"I have a feeling that we won't see them again," Ross said quietly to his wife once they had found an ice cream parlour and were watching Annie devouring that delectable concoction to her heart's content, with eyes closed in ecstasy.

"Why do you say that?" Martha responded in surprise. "We can find a way to get across there … somehow. Can't we?"

"We have no way of knowing how far it is, in what direction and how we would have to travel," he said, a concerned look on his face. "I have a good deal of work to do to keep the farms functioning in a very difficult market, and we've no idea how quickly this 'condition' will assert itself in Dad's lungs. And then we will have two nippers to contend with. How can you traipse them halfway across Europe at their age in a metal box for hours on end?"

"I see what you mean," she agreed. "But Annie *needs* her grandparents."

"This could be the *last* time we see them realistically," he went on as he wiped Annie's mouth of excess ice cream and lifted her into his arms. "On our way home then, my little one?"

"Yes, Daddy," she agreed, snuggling close to his chest. "Been joyed it. Will we see Nanny and Grandpa again tomorrow?"

"Don't think so," he replied. "They are away now on

holiday for a few weeks, so we will have to see when we will meet them again."

"Anyway, our carriage awaits so let's away home," Martha suggested. "Tomorrow's another day."

"Ay up, George!" Ross greeted his Garside Farm manager. "All rayt?"

"Aye, Ross," George returned as he strapped his Shire into his wagon shafts ready for his round. "Just about to bring our Maisie round to yours. Is that still all rayt?"

"Course it is, Owd Cock," Ross agreed. "But I thowt tha wor a rayt daft bugger for tekkin' yon nipper wi' thi on thi round t'other day. Owt could have happened. We were all worried, including Poppy. What's up, then?"

"Poppy and I have parted company," George answered.

"I rather gathered that, but what's tha doing about it?" Ross queried. "Has tha given up? Chucked all thy had with her away? Hasn't thy talked it through with her? I'm sure there will be room for compromise. And before thy goes on about differences, I know about your wedding plans, or lack of 'em."

"I've been ridiculously busy—" George stammered. "So—"

"Haven't we all in this hostile business environment, old man," Ross interrupted sharply. "Is there no room in thi 'ead to work things out wi' her? Or can't tha be bothered? Tha does love her I assume?"

"Unquestionably," George insisted. "But I'm not sure she'll have me back."

"I would advise thee to work out some possible dates when you might be wed," Ross suggested. "Take 'em to her and get her to decide. It's t'onny way. We've all been through this. Look what happened with our Joseph and his. Now you couldn't squeeze a tanner between 'em."

George fell silent, a deep look of concentration in his eyes.

"Shall I take Maisie back with me?" Ross asked as he turned to retrace his steps back to Boulders Wood.

"Martha's already been," George said. "She says that Annie has already missed her."

"Cap in hand, George, I would take thissen off to our Poppy today before she's off to her book signing in Richmond on Saturday," Ross advised. "It *will* work, mark my words."

With that the two men parted company – Ross back to Boulders Wood after his two hours in the meadows with Jim Smallshore and his flocks, and George on his way to Northallerton's railway station to send his produce off to the many stations in their area for collections to be delivered to his customers.

CHAPTER 11

Poppy sat down in her favourite easy chair by her most favourite wood-burning fireplace, with a sigh. How lovely to be back home after—

"A wonderfully exciting and thrilling day, don't you think, Poppy Spence, very successful author of romantic novels?" Abigail declared, already stretched out on the very comfortable settee. "Let's have a think while Hal, my wonderful husband and father to our little angel Grace, makes some tea."

"What did you think about the turnout at Blueberry's Bookshop?" Poppy asked nervously.

"Slow to start with," Abigail ventured slowly. "Particularly that first hour up to noon. I don't know whether you had time to notice, but after one o'clock, the queue was outside the door and down the street. I think that in total we must have sold close to five hundred books."

"Goodness gracious me!" Poppy said with a gasp.

"Five hundred and twenty-one!" Hal shouted from the kitchen. "We are assured that the avid readership that frequents the bookshop, that couldn't make it today, have left another one hundred and ten books on order."

"Well over six hundred then?" Poppy gasped, more than pleased with her day's work. "Will that be all, do you think?"

"Bearing in mind that this was your 'home ground'," Hal said as he brought in crockery, the huge steaming China tea pot, and a tray of cakes he found in the pantry. "We feel that the book is so good, it will do equally well wherever it is launched."

"London next stop in one week's time, eh?" Abigail announced. "Tell you what? How about going out for a meal to celebrate?"

"Not really," Poppy replied. "I am quite tired. How about you two doing that and I'll stay here with Grace, and then you can come back whenever you wish?"

"We can't do that without you!" Hal insisted, not wishing to put on their friend in such a fashion.

"Yes, we can," Abigail agreed with her friend, persuaded by her vigorous nodding. "Thank you, Poppy. That would be wonderful."

As soon as Grace had been put to bed in her own Cottage bedroom and had fallen asleep halfway through Poppy's story, Abigail and Hal set off for their favourite restaurant in Northallerton to enjoy and celebrate in style. It was particularly exciting for them as they hadn't done this sort of thing for as long as their daughter had joined them in their new life.

Almost immediately their carriage had disappeared through the gates, a gentle rattle of the door knocker alerted her to an unexpected visitor.

"Hello?" she called before deciding it might be safe to unlatch. "Who is it?"

"It's me – George," a very familiar voice greeted her.

She hesitated, unsure about what she ought to do, and then unlocked the door hurriedly and took one step backwards before allowing him to enter.

"George!" she declared, unsure how to greet him after their parting several days before. "Please come … in. Tea?"

"May we sit and talk first, Poppy? Please?" he asked slowly.

She ushered him into the sitting room and directed him to what had been his favourite place on the settee.

"What—?" she started, a little embarrassed.

"How—?" he blurted out at exactly the same moment, causing them both to giggle slightly.

"You first, George," she offered. "I've not heard your voice for ever such a long time."

"I was going to say, 'How do I start?'" he added haltingly. "First, I feel I need to apologise for the way I have treated you over the last year or two."

"There is no need—" she butted in.

"Please," he carried on. "There's such a lot I need to say. It's been very rude and incredibly stupid of me to fob you, of all people, off with a lame excuse for not setting our wedding day when you have asked me time after time. I have loved you for so many years that it should have been my first priority."

"And I shouldn't have treated you as *I* did, too," she added, shuffling closer to him, but still without contact.

"If there is time for me to make reparation for both my inactivity and my treating you unacceptably rudely, I have been setting out a few dates when we might possibly arrange our wedding date – if you still want me as your husband, that is," he suggested.

"I don't need an answer now," he added as he got up to leave, handing her a small sheet of paper. "But I would dearly like you to think about things and reconsider my urgent request for you to become my wife."

"George, I—" she replied, about to explain her situation concerning her book launches and signings. She remembered the last time she and Florence had left him with no explanation about their Grand Tour several years before.

"Could we perhaps meet sometime next week?" he asked as he made for the door. "Please?"

With that, he was gone, striding out purposefully across the field towards his home, leaving her no chance to answer.

She locked the door and plumped her backside once again on the settee where he had been sitting. Did she *really* believe he would find it easy to change his attitude and approach to her if she were to accede to his wishes? Did she really wish to become involved with him again in any shape or form? Once married, always married. Then there would be the question of children. What if…?

The front door clicked unexpectedly, startling her again. The vestibule door opened slowly and quietly, letting in…

"Abigail and Hal!" she retorted. "Haven't you been anywhere?"

"Certainly have," he responded jovially. "It's three hours since our departure to the most wonderful meal we have had for a long time."

"You looked shocked, dear Poppy," Abigail noted. "Seen a ghost?"

"Not quite … but close," she said with a nervous smile. "George came round to ask me if I would reconsider our position."

"And…?" Abigail retorted, a concerned frown decorating her forehead.

"He didn't stay long but gave me a list of dates when we

might reconsider a 'wedding day', if I would still accept him," Poppy explained. "Then he left in the hope that I would reconsider, choose a date, and speak to him next week about it. I think he's probably had advice from someone like Uncle Ross. I've known him long enough – thirty years or so - to know that he doesn't work out stuff like that rationally on his own."

"Next week?" Abigail said with a disbelieving shake of her head. "*Will* you reconsider his offer, and *will* you give him a date?"

"I … do … not … know, Abigail!" Poppy's answer came slowly and quietly. "Next week would be a non-starter anyway. Won't we be off to London early?"

"Certainly will!" Hal butted in. "Late Monday afternoon. You can't just drop into the metropolis in ten minutes. I mean, *really…!*"

"You need to speak to him no later than Monday morning," Abigail offered. "Do you really need all that aggravation again on your mind, especially during the time that could be pointing you towards the success and recognition you have always desired and deserved?"

"How's Grace?" Hal asked.

"We had a lovely time getting ready for bed," Poppy said. "She's been asleep ever since halfway through our story.

"Will I need anything special, clothes-wise I mean?" Poppy continued. "It's not a looking-round holiday type of stay, is it?"

"Very different from the last time we were there," Abigail answered. "You know, with Florence? This time it's down to business, trying to persuade individual readers and organisations that your book – and any that might follow – are worth reading. We will know by the end of London whether it will be worth pursuing Paris and Rome."

"Have we sent a copy to your relatives in those capitals?" Poppy asked tentatively.

"Indeed, we have," Hal re-joined. "They all have significant English friends who not only live in those countries but also very widely over here – some of whom live within striking distance of Pritchard's Bookshop in London and surrounding areas. Would you believe one of Abigail's brothers is a book distributor around Leeds?"

"By the way," Poppy pointed out quite seriously as she turned towards Hal. "You haven't sent me a bill for your services … yet."

"Very true," Hal returned "What I thought was—"

"Here's *my* take," Poppy interrupted. "How about if we agree on your letting me have *regular* bills on costs you incur. The emphasis is on the word regular. Then we will agree also on a percentage of all books we sell. Say, 30%?"

"That's too much!" Abigail interjected loudly and forcefully.

"Then 30% is what it shall be," Poppy insisted. "So today, for example, your take will be 30% of the money raised on the five hundred and twenty-one copies we sold. I need to be able to trust you – Abigail – to agree on that?"

"I will prepare the paperwork tomorrow, my dear Poppy, and I *personally* will ensure our signed documents are legally binding," Hal promised. "That, then, will form the basis for all our events and sales."

"Excellent!" Poppy said, clapping her hands quietly. "Don't forget that I still have a significant pot of money banked for me by Grandpa Ross, and that won't deplete any time soon. If you need any money in advance for things like publishing, printing, the trips to Paris and Rome, don't forget to *ask*, and it will be there forthwith."

"Do you really want to know your likely father, my son?" Jenny Bott asked Toby when Jonas was on one of his regular appointments at their local hospital.

"It is still important to me, even if it can't be substantiated," the lad stated quite categorically. "Every eighteen-year-old needs to know his sire."

"Come over here and sit by the fire with me?" she suggested. "Had I not sold my body as I did, I would not have survived to this age. Having no job meant there was no money coming in, and I couldn't rely on my father for help because, like you, I had no idea who he was. So, I had no option but to follow my mother into her line of work.

"Unfortunately, when I was twelve, she was stabbed through the heart by a drunken customer. He was carted off to jail and she was carted off to the mortuary. Alone at twelve, I had no choice but to carry on or starve to death.

"When I was sixteen I 'met' and mated your father who was a wealthy farmer – I say 'was'. Unbeknown to me he died in an accident on his farm, just before I was about to reveal your existence to him. His name was Mr Joss McIntyre, who owned Boulders Wood Farm, not too far from Richmond in the North Riding."

"Wasn't Mr Jamieson a distant relative of this man?" the lad questioned her in surprise.

"I believe so, but we have no proof, although he mated me several times – the dirty old bugger," she went on. "I tried to get our just recognition, but to no avail, and now I don't want Jonas to know, because he might just stir up a hornets' nest against us if he were to run with it – if you'll pardon the pun. He has enough money to allow us all to be comfortable for the rest of our life. Understand? *Understand!*"

"Yes, Mother," Toby answered. "I will keep it to myself. Promise."

CHAPTER 12

"Charity," Poppy greeted George's sister at their farmhouse front door early Monday morning. "Is George anywhere about?"

"'Fraid not, Poppy," Charity responded quickly. "You've just missed him, and he won't be back until this evening."

"We were supposed to be meeting very soon, but I won't be here for the rest of this week from tomorrow, as I am launching **Faithfully Yours** in London on Saturday," Poppy explained. "Would you be able to give him this note?"

"Of course, I will," Charity replied. "Does he need to reply?"

"Not really," Poppy answered. "The note should be self-explanatory."

As she reached Wisteria cottage, she noticed Hal's carriage and two outside the front door, with both husband and wife waiting in the living room.

"Poppy!" Abigail whooped as her friend hung her coat up in the entrance hall and made for the kitchen, to be halted by both her friends. "Kettle's already on, by the way. Sit down, please. Do you want the good news or the ... *really* good news?"

"Your choice," Poppy said, sitting down. "I'm just dying for a cup of tea and a really rich tea biscuit."

"The good news is that we've received a wire from our London contact to say that all is ready for Saturday," Abigail assured her.

"And the *really* good news?" Poppy giggled, expecting something really funny, as she could see her friend sniggering behind her gloved hand.

"Blackberry Bookshop in Richmond has just received a very large order from a local supplier," Abigail gushed as she burst into a fit of giggling that drew a smile from her husband. "Take off time, I believe, Miss Poppy Spence!"

Poppy settled back into her chair, flabbergasted that *her* book was now in such high demand, and that her dearest wish was beginning to become fulfilled. She gasped in awe, being brought back to earth with a bump when Hal rattled the teacups and three plated, each containing a luscious-looking slice of Mary's Victoria Sponge Cake.

"There are only two people in the world that can make such gloriously fresh-smelling Victoria sponge," Poppy shouted, "and I am sure that either one or both now inhabit my kitchen."

Everyone burst into fits of raucous laughter as both Mary and her niece, Mary-Jane sidled into the sitting room, each with a cup of tea and a side plate with a slice of cake.

"Mary! Mary-Jane!" Poppy gasped, jumping from her seat to hug them. "It is wonderful to see you both."

"We're here as a joint celebration, really," Mary announced. "We are thrilled that you are finally filling shop bookshelves with your beautiful novel, and here we have a boxful of your books that at least thirty of our customers have requested. Could you please be ready to sign and dedicate them to the list of people you will find inside the box, either now or when you come to the teashop on Saturday."

"Saturday?" Poppy puzzled. "But aren't we—?"

"Mary has asked that you come along to a book signing in her tearooms that she has been asked by many of her customers to arrange," Hal explained. "You see, people in this area consider you as one of theirs and as such want to be able to celebrate your success with you. We have enough time before we need to catch our train later in the day."

"And the other celebration is probably involving Mary-Jane?" Poppy suggested.

"No getting by you, eh, my dear Poppy?" Abigail warned with a nod.

"I have asked Mary-Jane to manage the shop next to Mary's Pantry that we have acquired," Mary went on to explain. "It will be on a part-time basis until the shop takes off. The rest of her time she will carry on for Mr Ross and Mrs Martha Booth at Boulders Wood. We have also another shop we are taking on. *That* we are leaving her to organise and arrange for opening at some time in the near future. How that is done will be entirely up to her. There. Done!"

"So, this is a double celebration of the success that two smart young women are and will be enjoying showing to the world in their separate fields in this area of Yorkshire's North Riding," Abigail announced, raising her cup of tea in salute. "I give you Mary-Jane Richardson and Poppy Spence."

"Cheers!" they all shouted in glee.

"Did you realise that significant numbers of our pheasants, partridges and rabbits are disappearing on a regular basis?" Ross informed his brother over one of their regular lunch breaks.

"How on earth did you work that one out?" Joseph guffawed, not believing a word of it. "Have you counted them?"

"Do you remember a chap we employed called … er … Jim Smallshore?" Ross asked sarcastically.

"Don't be stupid! Course I do," Joseph replied. "Well?"

"Part of his duties at this time of year is as a sort of gamekeeper," Ross explained. "He has noticed a significant decline in all the aforesaid species, and that can only be down to … poaching."

"Have you noticed any of this yourself?" his brother asked.

"Impossible to judge unless you have observed over a lengthy period. In this respect I have always trusted Jim's judgement," Ross added with a concerned look in his eyes. "And now we must do something about it."

"And the answer is?" Joseph queried, not really following his brother's reasoning. "Isn't it going to cost us?"

"The outlay will be negligible, and once we have the bugger, that's when we can start to recoup our earlier losses," Ross reassured him. "All we need to do is to release Jim from his present duties – we can cover those for a short time – and redirect him to become nature's sleuth to find out what's going on. Simple."

"Is he up for it?" Joseph asked. "*I* certainly wouldn't know where to start."

"We have talked, he and I, and he suggests spending part of each day trailing through our lands watching out for activities, trespassers, traps laid," Ross advised. "He thinks it would be best to alter the times of day to perhaps catch the poacher or poachers in the act, so he/they might be 'persuaded' to cease those activities."

"Sounds like a plan," Joseph observed as he stood up to return to his daily toil. "When should he start?"

"He already has and has found one rabbit trap so far – a wire noose," Ross pointed out. "The sort that has been in use since wire was invented.

"We sell quite a few rabbits to our local butchers, so this detective work will eventually make a significant difference," Ross remarked. "I just hope I don't find this thieving bugger before you do."

"Afternoon Ross, Joseph," a familiar voice accosted them as they began their return to work.

"Talk of the devil!" Ross said with a triumphant smile as he spun around. "Jim Smallshore. Good to see you. Hands full, eh?"

"These beauties are from our usual traps," he returned, holding up four fat but dead rabbits in his right hand." These others are … not, and you will notice that some on 'em are young 'uns, mekkin 'em too small to catch. Wire traps ower by t'lake – obvious as you like. Don't know who t'bugger is … yet, but I *will* sure as hell before long. T'last trap I found hadn't been set properly, so I can onny think I wasn't far behind him."

"Excellent work, Jim," Ross said, verbally slapping him on the back. "Had your dinner break yet?"

"Not yet," Jim said.

"Then for goodness' sake get thissen off 'om and take one of the proper sized conies for thi tea as I know you're a bit partial to a spot o' rabbit," Ross said with a guffaw.

"I am that!" Jim grinned. "Si thi Ross, Joseph."

"I am glad we brought him back from t'East Coast when

we did," Ross declared as he and his brother parted company to go their separate ways.

"Hasn't he started seeing somebody in t'village?" Joseph threw over his shoulder.

"Aye," Ross returned. "I believe it's yon Alice Jones, Peter Jones's widow. Well-matched I'm told by his daughter, Sally. Has tha been taking an interest in other folk then, Brother? About time."

As they disappeared around different corners of Boulders Wood House, a single horse carriage with three people inside – one much smaller than the other two – slowed to a stop outside Wisteria Cottage next to that belonging to Hal. The man dismounted and tethered his black shire outside the front door to the cottage, and helped the woman and small youngster down, ready to enter the cottage. He rattled the door knocker vigorously to alert the incumbents as to their presence. There was a brief hiatus before the door opened slowly and a young woman appeared.

"Father! Sally!" Poppy gushed as she ushered them inside. "And this must be … Annie. How lovely to see you all."

Mary had heard the greeting and beckoned Mary-Jane into the kitchen to make another pot of tea that the visitors might share, along with those glorious slices of Victoria Sponge. By the time the new visitors had settled, tea and cake had arrived ready for shared consumption.

"We felt we had to come along to congratulate you on your success with the book, and to buy one for ourselves," Sally said with a smile.

"Delighted!" Poppy enthused. "But no charge to family and close friends."

Conversations continued unabated until mid-afternoon when Abigail and Hal and Grace took off back home to finish their packing ready for the London trip.

"Wanted to let you know as well that I have been persuaded to join my practice with a much larger one, making our situation much more stable than before," Poppy's father announced.

"Excellent news," Poppy said in congratulation. "Does that mean you'll be moving?"

"Oh no," he retorted, flinging his hands in the air. "Staying where we are, but it does mean that we can make the one or two alterations necessary to bring the building up to date."

"Much as I'd love to stay, I have to pack for my next book launch in London this coming Saturday," Poppy explained.

"We also wanted you to be the first to know that my dear Sally is carrying little Annie's sister ... or brother ... to be delivered sometime early in the new year," Tommy Spence informed her, drawing his dear wife close to him as they made to climb into the carriage.

The look of utter delight and excitement that invaded Poppy's face told them how she felt about this news. Another sister? How wonderful!

George was utterly stunned to read the note Poppy had left for him earlier in the day when he had been out on his rounds. The letter read:

'Good morning, George. I am sorry I missed you, but I had already prepared this note in case you were out on your rounds.

'It was good to see you the other day and to be able to read what you had to say about your feelings, and to allow me to make a choice between certain days and dates for a 'possible' wedding day.

'It was interesting but not essential because, I feel, this needed to be done face-to-face a long time ago for me to believe in your sincerity. I feel that *I* must take my time to think seriously about your offer and to decide whether it is something I really would wish to do.

'I will be away for the next two weeks in London, finally to launch my novel "Faithfully Yours". Bit of an ironic title, really, don't you think, given the circumstance?

Poppy'

This note brought back very uncomfortable memories for him, taking him back to the time Poppy and Florence had departed on their 'Grand Tour', pushing him into making the hasty decision to marry the wrong person. Now what was he to do? Try to force the issue with her, when he knew she wouldn't be forced? Wait, to find out her decision had already been made? Caught between Scylla and Charybdis this time?

He needed to get on with his own life, working and looking after little Maisie, until he received her decision. Not sure how *that* was going to work.

CHAPTER 13

"Déjà vu," Poppy gushed once they were seated in the First-Class carriage on their train to London.

"Sorry?" Hal queried, not sure what she had said. "Daygeevoo? What's that?"

"It's French, my dear Hal," Abigail explained with a giggle. "And it means 'already seen'. It's used usually by people in a place they *feel* they have been to before. It's usually just a feeling that you've been there already."

"Except that this time, it's real," Poppy clapped her hands quietly, remembering the last twice – the first time as a twelve-year-old with her four dearest friends on the way to Yorkshire's East Coast with Nanny Nell and Grandpa Ross. That was a wonderfully exciting and adventurous holiday, but sadly two of those friends no longer are with her in this world, and from another she has become estranged.

The second time, their exciting Tour was undertaken with Hal and Abigail and her lovely friend Florence around a decade later, whom she had known since they were eight together at their first Christmas family gathering at Boulders Wood. What wonderful times she experienced as a young lady growing up!

"I was just reminiscing about our Grand Tour. What an excitingly wonderful time that was, and it was all down to you two. Both Florence and I were thoroughly captivated by all that you did for us," Poppy continued quietly, falling silent as memories of her dear friend filled her mind and her heart.

"She would have loved to have done this," she added after a moment of sad reflection and the shedding of a tear or two.

"She wouldn't have wanted tear-shedding or sadness because she enjoyed our travels just as much as you did," Abigail pointed out. "And now, something different; something that you were both aiming towards and would *both* have achieved."

"How do you think Saturday's event will work out?" Poppy asked, changing the topic gently.

"Rather like the one you did in Blueberry Bookshop, I should think," Hal said. "Pritchard's was set up as a bookshop in the late 1790s in Piccadilly, which has been the favoured place for booksellers since the 1890s."

"It is, however, on a grander scale undoubtedly," Abigail added. "This time we have ordered quite a few more books from the printer who will supply and deliver to the bookshop. Any we don't sell will be sent to the supplier to be saved for the next event. It all depends on our performance in London. I have written an article for The Times which will appear in tomorrow's edition. I have pulled out all the stops to bring in the hoards to Pritchard's on Saturday."

"Will I be able to cope with all this?" Poppy gasped, not sure whether she would be up to it at all. "Our signing at Mary's Pantry was beyond my wildest dreams in that I never expected all those people to come along to buy one of my books. It felt like Mary Ann Cross – otherwise known as my favourite author George Eliot – Louisa May Allcott and Georges Sand were all looking over my shoulder at the same time. I feel so sure that it wouldn't have happened had I not had you two to guide me along. I can't thank you both enough."

"No need, dear Poppy," Abigail assured her. "Those thanks are all reciprocated, because *we* wouldn't be able to enjoy the things we love without meeting *you*."

"And don't forget," Hal butted in, "that you and I, my dearest Abigail, wouldn't now be husband and wife, let alone have our little angel to *Grace* our lives."

They all laughed at Hal's clever pun before deciding to try the train's theoretically exquisite cuisine.

"Will we be using the same hotel in London as during our Grand Tour?" Poppy asked before Abigail and Hal retired with Daughter Grace. "The Grosvenor Hotel, wasn't it?"

"Indeed, we will," Hal agreed as he picked up little Grace's almost-sleeping body. He cradled her against his chest, whereupon she fell immediately into a deep slumber from which she would not stir until around seven o'clock in the morning, hence the reason for their trundling off to bed in good time.

The First-Class sleepers on the train were indeed that — comfortable and very luxurious and expensive. No problem for Poppy because her Grandpa Ross had left a significant amount of money in the bank account he had set up to cover all costs incurred with her writing projects. He didn't want her not to be able to continue with her passion because of lack of finance.

Although comfortable and well-appointed, once in her sleeping quarters, she couldn't get out of her mind her last meeting with George and how she had left the business between them, along with the impersonal note she had left with his sister, Charity. What would he do? Would he be able to understand the reasoning behind her words and, more to the point, would he be able to accept them?

Drifting in and out of Poppy's restless, disturbed sleep, Peter Olleranshaw wandered at will, turning up when least expected, and drawing her towards some unforeseen and inexplicable conclusion. What did these disturbed and disturbing images mean?

A watery early morning sun hailed their approach to King's Cross Station as she prepared herself for breakfast and the day beyond. Wednesday would give them all the time they needed to prepare for what they hoped would be an excitingly fulfilling approaching weekend.

"Mammy?" little Grace asked slowly as they sat in the dining car over breakfast. "Why are we not moving anymore, and why are all those people walking past our window?"

"Well, my little dear, we are on a steam train as you know," Abigail started to explain after they had all smiled at the little one's sharp observations. "We have stopped because we have arrived in London, and we thought you might like a bit to eat before we leave this lovely train."

Grace stopped talking as she chewed her breakfast slowly, looking around all the while.

"We will be leaving to find our hotel in a while, once we have finished eating," Hal said. "*Have* you finished eating?"

"Nearly," she drawled slowly as she chewed more slowly than before. "There. Finished. Don't want no more."

"Don't want *any* more," Abigail corrected.

"Don't *you* want no more either, Mammy?" Grace butted in, to the amusement of Poppy and Hal.

"Well, well, well," the deep gravelly voice resounded in the near empty hallway. "You *are* in something of a state, aren't you?"

"And who invited you here?" the owner of the empty

hallway snarled sharply. "And more to the point, why? We were supposed to have parted company a long while ago."

Well, you see, it's this way," the intruder sneered. "I am in need of some of that cash you *took* from me during our last job, and I thought you might be willing to reimburse it … fairly."

"And if I don't?" the other man replied, unthreatened by his words.

"I will remove you from that wheelchair and—" the new character threatened, taking a step towards him.

He moved no further as the man in the wheelchair reached under his seat to retrieve a Browning 190 semi-automatic pistol and, pointing it at the intruder, he said, "You were saying, Old Chap?"

Not expecting this, the intruder turned sharply and beat a hasty retreat towards the front door and freedom, warning an accomplice en route to do the same.

"Any tea on the go, my beautiful lady?" he shouted to his wife in the kitchen. "I could *murder* a cuppa."

"Who was the visitor?" she called back, conscious of a muted conversation.

"Oh, some beggar wanting a penny for a meal," he replied jovially. "I sent him away with a copper or two and a bit of advice."

"You are such a kind man," she shouted back. "I am glad you married me and no-one else."

"Me too, my sweet," he said, as he beckoned to his lad to join him in the living room, whilst crossing his lips as a sign of silence. "Would you like to come and give me a hand with my new wooden peg leg, old man? A bit more practice and I'll be walking again, hey what?"

The lad grinned as he pushed his stepfather's wheels while retrieving the false leg from a cupboard under the stairs. He loved being of use to this man who not only gave purpose to his life, even though through nefarious means at times, and who gave him a surname he had never had before. Made him sound like a real and acceptable person.

"Bear in mind, Old Chap, that we now have no need to work for a living," he said quietly to the lad. "However, we have to be on our guard to be able to protect what we have. There are some unscrupulous criminals out there who would dearly love to strip us of our wherewithal to lead a deservedly comfortable and respectable life. One day, perhaps, the blackguard that did this to me just might get his comeuppance."

"How bloody stupid and short-sighted are you, George Garside!" he muttered to himself in the cold living room, as the darkness closed around him. "She's rayt and you've missed another chance to marry the lass you were allus supposed to wed."

"Is that you, George?" his sister Florence's voice echoed down the stair well from her bedroom door. "George?"

"Aye, lass, it's me," he retorted, almost lapsing into depression at the deep mistakes he had made with the love of his life.

"Cup of tea?" Florence's voice piped up relatively cheerfully as she joined him. She was no lover of darkness or cold, so she turned up the gas mantles and pulled her thick woolly dressing gown closely about her. It was late spring but relatively warm weather never seemed to approach this area of Northern England until much later into the summer. Hardy beings these North Ridingers!

"Aye, lass. Go on then," he mumbled as he parked his backside non-too-gently into his usual easy chair. "Does tha know, Our Lass, I'll never learn."

"About what, then, Our George?" she replied as she brought in a wooden tray from the kitchen that had seen better days. Balancing on the tray could be seen a very large and ancient dark brown tea pot accompanied by two large but different-sized mugs. "Women?"

"Aye," he said slowly, eyes and mind a million miles away, as he sipped his tea.

"Out of the three women you have ever been relatively interested in, only one survives," she said quite pointedly. "She doesn't seem to be overly interested in you though. I would have thought – knowing you – that it was none of her doing."

Although he accepted that, the truth of his thoughtless intractability didn't sit comfortably with him. Trust his sister's blunt Yorkshireness to lay bare his stupidity.

"She needs to have her own space, you know, Brother," Florence advised. He had to listen because of two very poignant facts – she was his older sister and ... she was a woman. "I understand perfectly her desires to have people read and enjoy her writings, because there is an excitement in constructing a story that has come out of your own head. I feel sure, though, that *that* is not the be all and end all of her existence."

"All right. I accept that, but am I expected to stand by and ... wait?" he said quietly with a pained look in his eyes,

"I would advise getting on with your life patiently, but with an awareness of her *marital* needs," Florence explained. "I feel sure that in the near enough future they will show themselves, and you need to be aware, be there and be ready."

"I don't ... know," he muttered, still believing he had lost Poppy through being an ordinary chap leading an unexciting ordinary life.

CHAPTER 14

"Today's the day," Abigail warned Poppy over breakfast in The Grosvenor Hotel, a look of excitement in her face. "We will be in the firing line in two and a half hours, and now it's half past seven."

"I'm not sure about this at all!" Poppy returned nervously. "What if … nobody turns up?"

"What if nothing!" Hal tried to reassure her. "We have been told on good authority, by the organising bookshop, that there will be lots of folk wanting your book. Besides, I've seen the publicity and—"

"My article went in Wednesday's Times," Abigail reiterated as she handed over a copy of the newspaper, folded back to reveal the said article. Poppy took it and gave it a perfunctory glance.

"Yes, but…," she went on unconvinced by the 'proof' that Abigail had attempted to provide. "That doesn't guarantee there will be anyone walking through the bookshop's door specifically to buy one of my lowly stories."

"Trust me, Poppy," Hal countered. "I'm a McIntyre, and McIntyres know these things. Why don't we finish this divine breakfast, get ready and take a short walk to the book emporium where everything will have been set up with little to do other than to dedicate and sign your books, and speak a few words of encouragement to your prospective readers."

"I wonder if George—?" Poppy muttered almost absent-mindedly.

"Shouldn't worry about dear George," Abigail advised her. "I am sure he will be thinking about you and wishing you well."

Poppy stood up without a word, and ambled off to her room, ostensibly to prepare herself for the busy day ahead – they hoped.

"Never seen our girl so nervous and lacking in confidence before," Hal said to his wife, his frowning brows showing his concern. "Could it be anything to do with George, do you think?"

"Who knows?" she said, unsure of what to do or say that might help Poppy to overcome her nervousness and negative thoughts, "Let's hope she arrives at the bookshop on top form for today, or there would be no point in pursuing Paris … or Rome, or anywhere else for that matter."

"It'll be all down to you, Old Girl," Hal replied with a shrug and a sigh. "I need to stay with our Grace with perhaps a little walk in Hyde Park, maybe? It's only a short stroll from Pritchard's Bookshop down Piccadilly. There's also a new Lyons Tea Shop that was only opened in 1894 down here, that we might nip in to experience a morsel of their famous Treacle or Bakewell Tarts."

A quarter to ten," Hal announced flicking open his gold pocket watch attached to his waistcoat by a golden Albert, as they rounded the corner before approaching the bookshop. "My God! Look at that!"

The four of them halted abruptly as they noticed the queue of people stretching from the bookshop's front door, down the street to the next corner around which it disappeared. Folks were chatting jovially about books and things as they waited patiently for the bookshop doors to open.

As they neared the head of the queue, people stopped talking, turned, and pointed at Poppy.

"It's her!" the words shot down the queue. Some pointed at the larger-than-life photograph of the author on the inside of the shop's enormous window, along with her name, her book and the date and time of the signing.

"Hal?" Poppy gasped. "How did they get that ... that photograph?"

"Remember our Tour and my friendly little Kodak box camera with which I took all those photographs wherever we went?" he responded with a satisfied grin. "Well, *that* photograph is from *that* collection taken here in London by George Eliot's grave in Highgate Cemetery. I simply supplied the bookshop manager with the negative, and boom! Perfect poster for a book signing."

As they approached, a bout of cheering and applause greeted Poppy's arrival, and she acknowledged *that* with a wave and a huge grin of joy.

"I don't think we are going to have *any* problems with nerves or confidence at all," Abigail said to her husband. "That photo was a stroke of genius, my very clever husband."

Little Grace simply stood in awe at the number of people before her, as she couldn't take her eyes off the almost startling picture of her Aunt Poppy.

"Why is Auntie Poppy there?" she uttered boldly for her, stabbing her finger towards the shop window.

"It's so people will know who she is," her mother explained, her daughter's pert question bringing a smile to her lips. "Do you see all these lovely folks standing in this huge line here? Well, they have come to say 'hello' to her."

"Is that why we are here in L..O..N..D..O..N?" she asked slowly, not familiar with the name until very recently. "Will all the people in this town be here to say 'hello'?"

It was all that Hal could do to supress a smile to her very pointed question that he hoped could not be remotely possible. That would have meant a significantly long wait, and he was already feeling a little faint and light-headed from hunger, despite having eaten breakfast only an hour or so before hand. He was looking forward to his little walk with daughter Grace.

~⌁~

"Unbelievable!" Hal eulogised as they saw the last, happy book lover leaving the bookshop. "We must have dealt with anywhere between five and eight hundred sales."

"One thousand four hundred and eighty-two," Jerry Pritchard butted in. "Out of the batch that we ordered in, we expected to have quite a lot left to return to the supplier. However, we have only … eighteen! Magnificent, Miss Poppy Spence! Best we have ever done. Those eighteen will now go onto our shelves that I *know* will sell, along with another fifty we have ordered."

"You weren't here long, Husband, and you thought it was unbelievable?" Abigail asked.

"Actually, I was referring to the Sticky Treacle Tart that we had at Lyons Tea Shop!" Hal replied with a huge grin.

Poppy burst into a fit of laughter at his response.

"But this event, too, was something else," he went on. "Little Grace and I also had a wonderful time. Didn't we Grace?"

"Yes, we did, Daddy," Grace agreed. "I loved my Barking Tart, and my cup of tea."

"Barking…?" Abigail puzzled, nonplussed.

"Bakewell … Tart," Hal explained with a laugh. "Absolutely loved it!"

"You didn't…?" Abigail gasped with more than a little envy.

"What?" he said, a mock surprised look raising his eyebrows.

"Treacle Tart *and* Bakewell Tart?" she asked incredulously.

"Yes, Mammy. Daddy *did* have both," Grace piped in, sliding her arm through Hal's as he drew her to him. "And so did I!"

~

"And how are you feeling today?" Nell asked her husband at breakfast in their new luxury apartment in Nice. On the Front, looking out to sea, with an enormous, luxury balcony, they couldn't have chosen better, but this is what all his money had allowed them to do without worry.

"This outside space in the warm sunshine and fresh air is so invigorating," he replied as he sat at their new glass-topped table, sipping hot tea from new-fashioned glass tea mugs. "It almost makes me feel … alive again."

"What did yonder specialist say to you *this* time?" she queried, a worried frown decorating her face.

"Nothing too much to worry about when we have this—" Ross started to say, trying to give her a non-committal shrug. Unfortunately for him, she knew when he was trying to fob her off.

"Ross!?" she said firmly.

"Well … got perhaps fifty-fifty chance," he responded

almost off-handedly.

"Of what? Living until you're ninety?" she threw back at him sharply.

"Of making it to the end of this year, to be honest," he answered quietly.

His last words stopped her in stunned disbelief.

"But I thought you were getting—" she went on after a brief silence.

"Better?" he interrupted. "Like I say, touch and go."

"Well, is there anything we can do to make things better?" Nell asked, knowing really what his answer might be.

"I may well last until I'm a hundred," he offered. "But, then again, I might not last the week, I have to say, though that's the normal way of things for all creatures."

"So, what you are trying to say is that we should live our life as we would wish," she answered, "and—"

"Enjoy every second?" he butted in. "Too right … too right."

"Had a note from Ross this morning," Nell said, changing the subject, knowing full well there would be more to her husband's pronouncements than meets the eye.

"We need to get them over soon, perhaps?" he suggested.

"Won't happen," she went on. "Not for some time anyway. Problems with Poppy and George."

"Nothing too serious, I hope?" Ross said. "Anything we can do to help?"

"She doesn't want to marry him, probably because he has put off and put off setting the date," she said. "She can't wait any longer with his shilly shallying. Anyway, she's had two very successful book launches recently – one in Richmond and another in London."

"Pritchard's in London by any chance?" he suggested. "Piccadilly. Dates back to the seventeen hundreds."

"How on earth did you know that?" she puzzled, but knowing that there was always something he knew that she wasn't expecting.

"I have known Jerry Pritchard for a year or two," he went on. "And knowing that Hal had organised such an event, I dropped Jerry a line some time ago, and he wired me the result of the launch just after the event."

"Close on fifteen hundred copies of **Faithfully Yours**, Ross says," Nell explained. "Is that a lot?"

"A lot?" Ross returned. "That's an enormous number by anybody's standard. It should take her into the realms of George Eliot and Louisa May Alcott. Very few ordinary folks would be able to afford to buy such things."

"George Eliot? Surely that's a male name. Isn't it?" Nell observed with a frown. "Something Poppy didn't wish to be associated with?"

"Mary Ann Evans was a female author that assumes a man's name – George Eliot – because female authors weren't recognised as well. She married and became Mary Ann *Cross,*" Ross explained. "Poppy wishes to be known as Poppy Spence now, opposed to her original pseudonym/nom de plume P.P.Spence. It looks like that decision is about to pay off."

"Do you think there is ever a chance we may see her at some time in the future?" Nell asked, not holding out too much hope because of the distance. "If she only had wings!"

"I don't see any reason why not," he assured her. "Train journeys from Paris are regular and quite successful, I hear. Just need to look into their timetable. Leave it to me."

"The most important thing with you is not to tax yourself," she butted in. "I need you to stay alive, never mind aggravating your constitution."

"Peter?" Poppy said as she sat in the hotel's lounge with a cup of tea after Abigail and Hal had gone upstairs to put Grace to bed. A busy few days for all meant early to bed so they would be able to catch the morning train back home. Hal was sure that the seven hours or so that had become the norm for rail travel to the capital would change rapidly over the next year or two. Engines had become much quicker but would that the quality of the tracks and lines would follow suit!

"Poppy," a rather deeply gruff but polished voice accosted her. "How did the book launch go? Successfully I hope."

"I didn't know you were going to be here?" she said, a little embarrassed and taken aback by his suavely attractive appearance. Peter Olleranshaw's handsome face had captivated her from the moment Poppy had been thrust into his company over his copy editing her precious book and hadn't been out of her thoughts for very long since that time. "Yes, very successful indeed, I think you might say."

"I'm here on business, but could I get you a drink?" he asked, nodding at her cup of tea.

"Not really, thank you very much," Poppy answered him, feeling a little overwhelmed by his charm. "I'm not much of a beer drinker, really."

"I do have some Champagne on ice in my suite, if that might suit you better?" he replied, seeing she was hesitating more than a little. "A night cap perhaps, to celebrate a wonderfully successful day?"

"Well, perhaps so," she agreed almost eagerly. "It has been superb really."

"Good gracious!" Poppy gasped as Peter's suite door opened onto its magnificent splendour. "I've never seen anything like this!"

"Champagne?" he said smoothly as he helped her off with

her silk shawl and ambled into the bedroom to take off his dinner jacket and bow tie. "The flutes are by the settee and the bottle of Dom Perignon is still on ice there, too. Try the … settee. It's so—"

"Comfortable," she added with a sigh as she sank into its gloriously cushioned velvet.

"Cheers," he said softly, offering her a newly poured glass of expensive bubbles while sitting down close enough for her to feel the warmth of his body.

Her eyes closed gently, almost in ecstasy, a slight frisson of excited sexual apprehension coursed her young body, almost preparing her for what this man might offer her.

"Peter!" she gasped slowly and quietly as his arm slid effortlessly around her waist, drawing her unresisting body gently to his.

CHAPTER 15

"Nar then George, mi owd cock," Harry, one of George's customers of old on his North Riding round, greeted him. "Not sin thee for a while. Is thy all rayt?"

"Ow do, Harry?" George returned quietly, carefully looking about him in the place he had been stabbed by Jonas Jamieson. He half expected to see a shady figure lurking in the dark entries round about, and partly would have liked to see his nemesis so he could finish off their business once and for all. "Been ridiculously busy and have neglected my best customer to a certain extent – and then there's you."

They both burst out laughing as they shared the repartee they had enjoyed for many a year.

"Back to one delivery a week ifn that's all rayt wi' thee?" Harry responded. "Business these days isn't as good as it used to be. Fewer customers because of less money coming in. Tough times ahead, I believe. We are having to reduce our prices largely because prices from the *big* suppliers are dropping as tastes change, and we have to keep pace with our competitors."

"Except for folks like us," George butted in. "It's not so much that our prices are dropping as tastes change, it's that one minute folks are demanding corn and stuff, and the next minute, they want dairy. Things then become tight because foodstuffs seem to be on an upward spiral permanently."

"One day, eh, George?" Harry finished off as George moved towards his wagon. "Si thi next time."

"Aye, Harry," George replied as he moved off slowly, again making sure no dodgy characters were lurking in the maze of streets, snickets and alleyways roundabouts. "Si thi."

He made to turn a corner off the main thoroughfare and was sure he caught sight of a familiar figure being pushed along in one of those new-fangled wheelchairs made for folks as couldn't walk.

"Woah, lass!" he urged his shire, drawing his wagon to a halt. He leaped from his driving seat and rushed to the corner he had just turned, to look down the main street, to see … nothing. It was virtually empty, with only people hurrying home for tea and to escape the utter tedium of minimally paid humdrum work.

"Damn!" he snarled. "I could have sworn…!"

Although George quite enjoyed what he did for a living, the ultimate purpose had disappeared from his existence with his parting from the love of his life. He had made many mistakes as he had grown to manhood, the most glaring of all being not carrying Poppy along with him. The two real glaring errors had been choosing other women to become his wife, and both of these had proved to be only fill-ins in default of not having his true love to occupy his life. Now his chance of lasting happiness with her seemed to have escaped him forever.

How he wished he could look forward after a day's hard toil to sharing his evening time with his Poppy, without having to picture her elsewhere in the world meeting other like-minded people discussing her books. Had she also found someone else with whom to share *her* down time? This played on his mind constantly.

⁓

"No! No!" Poppy gasped in shock as she kicked off the bed sheets and grabbed her clothes from the pile on the floor next to the foot of the bed. "I can't do this!"

Peter Olleranshaw's look of shocked surprise at her complete rejection of the close intimacy they were about to share, overwhelmed his face. How could this have happened? What had he said or done that turned her off in such a catastrophic way?

"What is it, Poppy?" he said quietly. "Was it something I did or didn't do?"

"I don't want to sleep with you, Peter," she snapped as she dressed hastily. "We are not married, and I … can't …have … sex … with you!"

She slammed out of the room in anger at herself, almost running to the safe haven that her own room offered her. How could she have allowed him to persuade her into his bed? She felt that this had been uncomfortably close to the violation of her once safely held desire to offer herself in marriage to the man of her dreams. Is that what Peter Olleranshaw was – the man of her dreams? Did she really want to be married to *him*? Was he, in fact, *offering* her marriage?

Trying to fit her key into the lock with an uncontrollably shaking hand, she dissolved into fitful sobs, realising what a close call that had been. She collapsed on the bed once her door had been locked safely behind her and knew no more.

⁓

The watery rays from a late spring morning sun crept between the velvety curtains of Poppy's bedroom, interrupting her preparation for breakfast. She had tried hard to thrust the happening of the night before from her active mind, but to no avail. How was she going to manage for the rest of the day in the company of her friends, knowing how close to disaster her feelings had brought her? Something, no doubt, that many a young woman had experienced before her, and something that she couldn't afford to let happen again.

"Good morning, Poppy," Abigail greeted her friend. "You are looking a little peaky this morning. Are you feeling all right?"

"Hal not here yet?" Poppy answered quietly, looking around almost to prove that he was nowhere nearby.

"He's upstairs seeing to Grace," her friend returned with a slight frown. "Any reason why you ask?"

Taking the opportunity to speak to Abigail while they were alone, Poppy explained the events of the evening before. Abigail listened quietly intent on what she was being told, with no intimation as to how she felt about what she was hearing. Once Poppy had finished her hesitant account, Abigail fell silent for a few moments, undoubtedly, to allow her to take it all in.

"I should have told you about his reputation and about his known desire never to wed," she started to say. "So, you have had a close call, my dear friend. It's a good job you didn't continue – you didn't … continue, I hope?"

"I did not!" Poppy denied vehemently. "I couldn't have – without suddenly becoming a hypocrite. I now want nothing to do with him, or even to be in the same room as him. Consequently, I should like you to sever all links with him forthwith. Could you do that … please? And could you not say a word to Hal?"

"Consider it done, my dear Poppy," Abigail assured her with a smile.

"Good morning, everyone," Hal greeted them cheerfully not three minutes later.

"Hello Mammy. Hello Auntie Poppy," five-year-old Grace piped in almost immediately. "I have just seen Mr Holleringshort on the stairs. He ignored Daddy as he rushed downstairs with his sweetcart."

"Suitcase, Darling," Hal corrected. "It's called a suitcase."

"Why is it called that, Daddy?" Grace asked as she shuffled in her chair up to the table.

"It's what gentlemen put their clothing – including suits – in so they can travel with a change of clothing," Hal explained.

"What does 'travel' mean, Daddy?" Grace asked. "Why 'travel'?"

"Steady, my girl. Steady," Hal gasped. "One at a time."

"We have travelled from our home to somewhere new, and that's what gentlemen and ladies do quite a lot," Hal began to explain to his daughter. "They used to put their belongings and clothes and stuff in a box called a trunk—"

"Did they keep their pet elephants in there as well, Daddy?" she asked very quickly. "It must have been a very big and heavy … trunk. Did they live in them, too?"

Hal cast a glance at the heavens and Abigail giggled at the picture thrust into her unsuspecting mind by her inquisitive little girl.

"No, my sweet," he replied patiently. "The gentleman would have someone else to move it for him. Anyway," he said moving on swiftly, "someone else decided to make something much smaller that the gentleman could carry himself to contain a change of clothes if he was to be away for more than a few days. This was a box with a handle that became known as a 'suitcase' in which he could carry his belongings and clothes and a—"

"Suitable," Grace blurted out.

"Suit," her father corrected. "Good girl! Your usual breakfast?"

"Yes please," she responded in glee, clapping her hands quickly as her mother fastened a rather large white silky serviette around her front, "Scrammle eggs and bacon. Yum! Yum!"

The adults laughed at her enthusiasm for what she was about to dive into enthusiastically.

"Don't forget to eat it all," Abigail advised. "We won't be eating again for a while on the train."

Poppy sat in silence for a while picking at her food slowly, a distant look in her eye. She still bore the shock of last evening's events in Peter Olleranshaw's suite, very glad that *that* relationship had gone no further. Heaven only knows how she would have felt if it had travelled its ultimate course. Hearing an invisible and almost silent sigh of relief, she began at last to tuck into her breakfast heartily, looking forward to riding the train back home.

The return rail journey north brought back significant memories and thoughts surrounding her twelfth birthday celebrations up and down the new lines between Scarborough, York and Middlesbrough, and through the many beautiful villages en route to and from Yorkshire's starkly beautiful east coast. Poppy and her dear friends had been stunned on many occasions by the unexpectedly splendid, newly created Victorian buildings, some of which offered them luxurious rooms within which to glory in their unsought but enjoyed holiday by the sea.

"Penny for your thoughts?" Abigail offered quietly as she cradled her sleeping daughter in her lap.

"Just re-treading my twelfth birthday celebration that saw us travelling Yorkshire in one of those new-fangled early trains to visit Scarborough," Poppy returned. "Out of the five, only three of us survive, one of whom I haven't seen for many years."

"That wouldn't be George then, would it?" Abigail asked tentatively.

"No. That's a different story," Poppy responded. "Our dear friends Florence and Alice passed away a few years ago, and Alice's sister, Annabel, I haven't seen at all for a long time. It would be good to catch up with *her*."

"We've worked out all the details for your next launch," Hal said causing Poppy to prick up her ears while he flicked through his 'Bible' of a notebook.

"Please don't keep me in suspense, Dear Hal!" she urged, almost sitting stiffly to attention.

"Paris in two weeks," he replied almost off handed. "Same hotel as last time, and a bookshop called Librairie Garibaldi on the Rue de Rivoli, across from the Jardin des Tuileries."

"And what is that, pray?" she reacted quickly, puzzled at the name.

"Literally means 'Tile Factory Gardens'," he said with a self-satisfied smile.

"Tile factories built in a garden?" Abigail sneered. "You expect us to believe that?"

"Goes back to the times before the French Revolution when, in 1564 Queen Catherine de Medici had a *palais* or palace built on a large piece of land where there used to be tile factories – or tuileries," Hal began to explain in his serious voice. "In 1789 King Louis XVI and Marie-Antoinette were imprisoned there at the start of the Revolution. Not long after, the land became a public park, and has been so ever since."

"Why were they imprisoned there?" Poppy asked.

"As a precursor to a 'sharp' visit to Madame la Guillotine because they were the king and queen," he explained. "At this time of revolution, a lot of rich people and nobles were executed after them. Not a good idea to be rich during such events."

"The bookshop?" Poppy reminded him.

"Probably one of the earliest in France," Hal said. "Opened sometime round about the very early nineteenth century. Incidentally, we will not be visiting Rome this time."

"Oh? Why not?" Poppy asked. "I thought we—"

"We've decided to visit somewhere else in France," Abigail re-joined. "You have two choices. Either you could have it as a surprise, or we could tell you where we are planning to take you."

"I should like to know, please," Poppy said quietly.

"Well then, my beautiful wife will explain," Hal said, bowing to Abigail.

"Abigail?" Poppy reacted cautiously.

"We have decided to take a train ride to … see your Nanny and Grandpa in Nice," Abigail announced. "Trains these days are very quick, so we thought we would spend a fortnight visiting them where you will get the chance to spend a whole week in their company … alone."

Poppy almost stopped breathing as this news began to sink in - her face a stunned ashen colour as tears began to well.

"Breathe, Poppy!" Abigail urged. "Breathe. They *do* know and are extremely excited about the whole idea."

Poppy said not another word, but she broke down in sobs, her hands covering her face as her tears flowed.

Chapter 16

"So, *you're* the estimable George Garside," the young lady said sidling up to him as he unloaded his last call of the day before his lengthy journey back to his lonely, cold home.

"And who wants to know, Miss?" he replied almost with his back to her. "I don't think we've met before, but do I know you?"

"You certainly do," she responded quite firmly. "My name is Annabel, and you were once married to Alice."

"I still don't recognise you," he retorted. "If I *do* know you and you want me to believe you, tell me something about me that nobody else would know."

"Alice was my twin sister," the young lady replied.

"You look nothing like Alice," he scoffed.

"We were not identical," she came back at him. "I was slightly taller and a few minutes older. We also shared the same room in the Grand Hotel in Scarborough. You know, the one shaped like capital letter 'V'? V for Victoria?"

"Annabel," he sighed, taking her in his arms. "I'm sorry but I had to be sure. Where are you staying?"

"I *have* nowhere," she explained. "Mam and Dad died a while ago in a house fire, leaving me with no parents and nowhere to live."

"We have plenty of room at our farm," he offered. "So, you are welcome to come and stay with us."

"You said … we?" Annabel returned carefully. "Are you … married? Perhaps to … Poppy?"

"Not married," he said sadly. "I live at the farm with my sister Florence – who is an up-and-coming author – and my five-year-old daughter Maisie. *She* had a twin who died. They were the only children Alice and I had. Plenty of bedrooms, you see, for you to choose for as long as you need it. Do you work?"

"Had a job in a shop until it closed when the owner died," she said.

"Homeless and jobless, eh?" he smiled ruefully. "It so happens it's your lucky day because I have an opening in our dairy, if you're interested, of course."

"What about board and lodgings?" she asked tentatively, not sure about wages and whether she would be able to afford both.

"Good wages, and no charge for board and room," he chortled. "You're family, for goodness's sake!"

"Manna from the gods!" she exclaimed, kissing him on the cheek as he helped her into the wagon. "By the way, I can cook, too."

"Top of my chart, then, Annabel," he laughed, the happiest he had felt for a long time. How was he going to cope with having her living under the same roof as Alice had done? Would he be drawn to her, or would he be prepared to wait for Poppy's answers? He hadn't done that twice before and look what had happened.

They spent most of the homeward journey in a reasonably comfortable silence, broken gently by the occasional comment about shared experiences and company. They talked little about Alice, because each felt it might prove to be too raw even though she had been gone a number of years.

"Did Alice have the chance to spend any time with her children?" Annabel asked gently as they approached Garside Farm's outer entrance.

"Died in childbirth, I'm afraid, so, no," he answered quietly. "She didn't even get the chance to *see* them."

"I'm sorry," she whispered, putting her hand on his lap fleetingly as the wagon drew to a halt outside the main door.

The warmth of the interior drew a deep sigh of relief and contentment, and clawed back memories of the very few occasions she had visited during the short time her sister had lived there. Her marriage to George had set the two sisters apart to some extent partly because they had always been close as twins, but also because Annabel had considered it to have been precipitate and poorly thought through. She was now unable to set right the animosity that had divided them, which had prayed upon her mind of late.

"Annabel?" a light female voice floated down from the head of the stairs.

"Florence!" Annabel called back, elated to hear her voice. She had always liked Florence's no-nonsense approach to everything in life; calm, pleasant, non-argumentative and forever smiling.

"Just happened to see your brother as he was making his last delivery, and he offered me a lift," Annabel explained.

"Are you going on holiday?" Florence returned. "Suitcase?"

"Homeless, I'm afraid," she said. "Lost my job as well."

"Thank God!" Florence uttered with a degree of relief.

"We have so much spare space in here and a severe need for workers in our dairy. Are you—?"

"Available?" Annabel interrupted quickly, a relieved smile creasing her face. "Certainly am."

"Then the gods *have* heard my prayers," her friend responded excitedly. "And at last, another female voice to engage with."

"Maisie not here?" Annabel asked Florence as they made up the bedroom she was to inhabit for the foreseeable future.

"Sleeping over at Ross and Martha's place tonight," Florence explained. "Martha looks after her during the day to take pressure from George's shoulders. The little lass has a lot of upset lately, what with the death of her twin and the loss of her nanna. She's about the same age as *their* little 'un, Annie, and so their days are spent in splendid engagement. You'll be able to see her tomorrow. Your niece!"

⁓

"Auntie Martha?" Maisie asked in that liltingly questioning tone that most youngsters use.

"Yes, my lovely. What can I do for you?" her aunt replied as she tucked her in bed. "I'll do you both a story in a little while, if that's all right for you. It is, of course, my little one, your turn to choose which story."

"Thank you, but that's not what I wanted to ask," Maisie said with a slight wrinkling of her forehead. "Would it be all right to stay here?"

"Of course, it would," Martha answered. "You're staying until tomorrow evening, when your daddy has finished work. When he—"

"To stay here all the time, I mean," the child said pointedly.

Little Annie sat up in bed quickly, a huge smile decorating

her face. *She* understood perfectly what her cousin was asking, and so did her mother, a fraction later.

"Well can she Mammy?" Annie asked earnestly. "Please, Mammy?"

"I don't think so," Martha said gently, knowing what George would say. "Her daddy will want her back home at the end of each day, I'm sure."

"Would it be all right to stay with you all in the week and go home at weekends?" Maisie threw in smartly.

"We'll see what your daddy has to say," Martha responded on her way to their bedroom door. "Now off to sleep."

Later that evening she shared the children's wishes with her husband who was not in the least surprised.

"Is Maisie any trouble for you?" Ross replied over a cup of tea. "I mean, would it be a problem? I know our Annie is beginning to need nippers of roughly her own age around her – friends whom she gets along with and to whom she can relate."

"Often I don't know she's there, because she is so quiet and well-behaved," his wife returned almost with an air of puzzlement in her voice. "It's almost if she really needs to be here. The two of 'em are almost like sisters, and they never don't get on with each other. It would be no trouble to me, and I feel that our Annie *needs* her there."

"I'll speak to George tomorrow," Ross added. "It would probably be a god send to him because I know there is nobody to look after her as regularly as he works late. Leave it to me. He can always come and spend time with her when he's on a short shift."

"How are you feeling now ... Mrs Jamieson?" Jonas asked his new wife as he hobbled from the registry office to their new motor vehicle just a few steps and clumps away. His new wooden peg leg, although uncomfortable and slow, allowed him to stand and hobble about better than if he was in his wheelchair. He still felt significant animosity towards his arch enemy, George Garside. That would always be there, in his mind, but would take time to move slowly to the *back* of his mind. Perhaps his new life with his new family would help to change his anger towards him into a fading memory only.

"I don't know yet," his new wife responded with a giggle. "It all depends—"

"Well now," a gruff rasping voice accosted the pair threateningly. "Fancy meeting you here! I said we would meet again, and … here we are."

"And you are?" new wife snapped as she was helping her husband into the motor car, still having his walking stick to hand, and recognising the newcomer's menace from experience. "Get away!"

"Be careful, harlot!" the threatening voice warned. "If you're not careful, I will dispatch your spouse 'ere and show you what I think about you."

Without further annoyance from him, she swung the walking stick with deadly accuracy, wreaking significant damage to the side of his head, bringing him down into a gathering pool of his own blood. Her son finished the job with a hefty boot to the injury, ushering his mother into the back of the vehicle before climbing into the driver's seat and setting off for home.

"Magnificent!" Jonas cheered with a punch to the air. "My heroes, Jenny and Toby … Jamieson. Nobody will mess with us from hereon in. I didn't even have to lift a hand. Home Toby and don't spare the horsepower!"

Toby couldn't believe his luck at being able to drive this luxurious Lanchester Landaulette with its twenty-eight horsepower, purringly powerful engine. Jonas couldn't have attempted to do it because of his leg, and Toby's mother was never considered because she was … well … a woman. Jonas was unbelievably happy because not only did he have the wife of his dreams, but he had a remarkably smart and able 'son'.

"I could get used to this," Toby rejoiced, almost drooling over the thought once they were back at home. "When does the motor car go back?"

"It's not going back," Jonas assured him, much to the lad's surprise. "It's here for good. Ready for you to drive whenever necessary. You will be my chauffeur, old chap, for which I will pay you a princely sum. You will also have your own suite of rooms in which to rattle around. Unless you still would want to live with your mama and your stepfather, whoever he might be."

"Not sure about the last option," he joked, a smile on his lips. "I might even sleep in the motor car!"

He was interrupted by a sharp rattling of the door knocker, attended by the cry, "Open up! Police!"

CHAPTER 17

Poppy stood in awed silence as she gazed at the Rue de Rivoli in Paris's First Arrondissement, stretching from the Place de la Concorde to the Place de la Bastille, trying to take in the vista that obliged her to remain motionless and voiceless.

"Yes, dear Poppy, *that is* the next signing emporium," Hal stated quite categorically. "But not for a day or two. In fact, three days as today is mercredi.

"Merc—?" she puzzled, until it finally grabbed her. "Wednesday! French for Wednesday.

"What does Grace think about our present jaunt into another world?" Poppy went on as she lifted their daughter into her arms.

"I think it is … lovely, Poppy," Grace replied, more than a little forward in how she addressed her aunt. "I may call you Poppy, may I Auntie Poppy?"

"Of course, you may, Grace," Poppy responded with a nod and a smile. "After all, we are friends, are we not?"

"Indeed," the youngster returned to the smiles that Abigail and Hal felt they had to hide.

128

"Is there any reason why this street is called 'Rivoli', Hal?" Abigail asked. "Do you know?"

"Indeed, I do," he commented with a sage nod. She often acknowledged that her husband was a veritable encyclopaedia of nigh on useless information that she would often test him on. "It was named after Napoleon's victory against the Austrian army in 1797's Battle of Rivoli. You know of Napoleon, my sweet? Of course you do. This street also has a lot to do with the French Revolution as it stretches from the Place de la Bastille – starting place for the revolution – to the Place de la Concorde, where the Guillotine was stationed. It was originally called Place Louis XV but was renamed Place de la Revolution followed by Place de la Concorde."

"Why 'Concorde'?" Poppy asked, knowing little about such points in history.

"The name 'Concorde' means *agreement* in French, and was intended to herald reconciliation among the French people following the excesses of the Revolution's *Reign of Terror*," Hal finished off.

"Nervous?" Abigail asked Poppy.

"So so," she re-joined hesitantly. "Very different situation from London, I have to admit. I enjoyed our time here on our Grand Tour with Florence, but now …?"

"Very different feeling and possible outcome?" Hal pointed out. "More like an important part of your life that you've always looked forward to?"

"Yes," she returned after a moment or two's hesitation. "I feel like I'm here for the first time because we were so busy the last time following our brief of following in our heroes' footsteps, and didn't have the time to take in sights, sounds and smells of the place. This city looks so open, so vibrant and so alluring that I'd like to explore it all – every nook and cranny."

"We do have a spare couple of days, you know," Hal remarked. "We feel the same as you and we'd like to take Grace to see some of the overwhelming sights before you are thrust into the maelstrom of trying to persuade your audience that their life will never be the same unless they acquire a copy of **Faithfully Yours**, dedicated and signed by its famous author, Poppy Spence."

"Like to give it a whirl?" Abigail suggested eagerly. "I simply need to have words with the owner of Librairie Garibaldi this afternoon concerning the arrangements for Saturday…"

"And I need to plan our trail over the next two days, which shouldn't take too long," Hal added breezily.

"Then "Boom", we're off," they both chorused.

"Actually," Hal added quickly, "we have Sunday of this week too, because the train from Paris to Nice doesn't leave Paris until twenty to midnight, as we will be taking the Train Bleu overnight sleeper."

"Overnight?" Poppy gasped. "Why? How long does it take to get to Nice from here?"

"We will be at the Cote d'Azur by seven o'clock the following evening," he replied. Takes nineteen hours and twenty minutes all told. There is a diner on board, so we will miss nothing important. You will have a few surprises that will blow your socks off, but you will have to wait and see what they will be. You will be seeing your Nanny Nell and Grandpa Ross on Tuesday of next week – less than a full week away. How does that grab you?"

Poppy burst immediately into a flood of emotional tears at the thought.

"Hal!" Abigail urged her husband quietly, with a shake of the head and a warning frown.

"What?" he returned, not understanding what he had said that had caused such a sharp reaction. "I was only saying…"

"How is Annabel managing in the dairy, Florence? Charity?" George asked his sisters one morning before breakfast.

"Certain things she has to learn, I suppose," Charity returned with a non-committal shrug. "It's only to be expected after only a short time. She'll be rayt."

"How are *you* getting on with her?" she continued after a moment's hesitation, as if she didn't know what to say.

"I don't know what you mean," he retorted almost too quickly to be believed.

"I think you do. Come on, Brother!" Charity insisted. "Don't forget that I was around when Alice lived here. Again, I might add, when Poppy *wasn't* here. You keep defending yourself by denying any involvement, but you protested *that* the last time she wasn't around. Same place, I believe?"

George fell into an uneasy and uncomfortable silence, staring into the empty distance.

"She said she didn't want to carry on with me," he shrugged.

"And?" she pushed. "What else did she say in her note?"

"Note?" he defended quietly.

"'I must take my time to think seriously about your offer and to decide whether it is something I really would wish to do.'" Charity offered. "Now do you remember?"

"How did you know that? I thought it was a note for me!" George complained in embarrassment.

"It was screwed into a ball on the floor in the kitchen," she explained. "Fair game."

"She has better things to pursue than wait for a loser like me," he acknowledged, resigned to his fate. "I feel I need to get on with *my* life and stop trying to please other people."

"You've certainly not succeeded in doing that, my dear brother," Charity responded smiling ruefully.

"Thanks, Sis," he returned, unhappy with how their

conversation was moving.

"Morning everyone," a pleasantly lilting voice joined them at the breakfast table.

"Morning Annabel," Charity replied. "Ready to knock the dairy parlour into shape?"

～

"Good morning, Inspector Shaw," Jonas greeted the police inspector and his sidekick constable. "How can we be of service to you today?"

"We are still moving forward in our investigations concerning the theft of materials from Thresher Hall some time ago now," Inspector Shaw explained. "We would like to ask you some further questions to clear up a few queries we have."

"We'll need to take all your questions etc into the study at the back of the house," Jonas responded calmly. "They needn't concern the rest of the household. Toby? Can you get my wheelchair, please?"

"Certainly, Boss," the lad agreed, helping him to settle before wheeling him out of the front room.

"Why does Jonas need to answer questions about something he knows nothing about, Toby?" Jenny puzzled. "*Does he know anything about this?*"

"No idea, Mam," the lad said. "I wouldn't have thought so. They probably believe he knows someone that might have been involved. They often have to follow up what they consider might be the tiniest of leads to try to find a way forward. He'll see them off, have no fear."

The door opened with a bump and Jonas sitting in his wheelchair between the door jambes.

"I have to go to the police station, Jenny, Toby," Jonas

acknowledged. "They think I may be able to help with their enquiries. I won't be too long."

With that the constable swished the chair around and pushed him out to the police van quickly and with little ceremony. Once the outside front door had slammed shut, they heard the revving sound of the van's engine, and then … silence.

Mother and son were left stunned and very concerned that the police would either find something he would need to answer for, or he might have been arrested. Jonas seemed quite calm though, and that persuaded his wife that it might just be a formality.

"Do we need to consult the solicitor, do you think?" Jenny asked her son.

"Not until we get to know if he's been charged with anything," Toby answered with a sage nod.

Chapter 18

The front door snicked shut as the owner turned the key in its rather stout-looking lock. Five o'clock and the sun's light glistened on the very still and smooth surface of the River Seine.

He let out a very deep if contended sigh as he sat down next to a very small pile of books, an empty ink well and three very well used quill pens standing upright within its round body.

"Well, Miss Poppy Spence, you will no doubt see that we sold almost all of the books we ordered on your behalf," he advised her in his broken English. "I feel sure you must have – Ow do we say it? – writers' gamp?"

"I think that would be 'writers' *cramp*', Monsieur," Hal corrected him. "Not quite as many as in London last week, but still a significant number, bearing in mind this is not … London."

"What do *you* think, Poppy?" Abigail asked.

"A wonderful experience where I have spent time with some lovely people – both English *and* French," Poppy agreed.

"But I am now tired and would perhaps need to return to the Hotel Excelsior for a bath and ready myself for dinner. Did we do well, M. Henri?"

"Although mostly English people that either live here abouts or that spend their – how you say? – vacancies here," he replied.

"Would that be 'vacances' – holidays?" Hal said with a knowing smile, drawing his sleeping daughter to his chest.

M. Henri smiled, nodding vigorously, packing away the half dozen or so copies of Poppy's book as he explained how quickly they would disappear in the following day or two.

Abigail helped Poppy to her feet before they set off to cover the three hundred yards or so to the hotel's front door, to prepare for the evening.

"I will put your proceeds in your bank on Monday, Monsieur 'Al," the shop proprietor had promised. "I will also send you details of all sales within the next week or so direct to your 'ome."

~

"What a wonderful place and a super time I had with all those people!" Poppy eulogised as Abigail and her friend sat down for their meal.

"No Hal and Grace?" she asked.

"Hal's having room service after he puts Grace to bed," Abigail explained. "Bath first and then nice clean nightdress as father and daughter eat dinner together. You'll get to talk to him tomorrow about the next couple of weeks in the French Riviera."

"Two book launches in two capital cities!" Poppy gasped. "Excitingly wonderful, with only one downside with which I am sure you would agree."

She dropped her chin slightly, looking just under her lids at Abigail with a modicum of dismay.

"Well, he *was* handsome and – dare I say it? – attractive enough to have almost reeled you in," Abigail noted. "I can assume you will get over that slight mistake?"

"Already gone," Poppy agreed. "And I wish to have no further contact with him, thank you very much."

"Duly noted, my dear friend," Abigail agreed very firmly. "There is no earthly reason why we shouldn't decide which publisher to use in future, anyway. I feel sure there will be a veritable queue of organisations ready to take up the cudgels on your behalf. You really need to be aware that your success as a novelist and your fame now fly before you. Hence, the rest and relaxation you will enjoy with your Nanny and Grandpa Booth is very necessary to prepare you for your next instalments."

They fell silent for a few moments as they polished off their sizeable portions of Black Forest gateau swimming in doubly thick cream, leaning back afterwards in their chairs with a hefty sigh and semi-closed eyelids.

"That was—" Abigail almost gasped.

"Immense?" Poppy added with a nod of contentment. "We eat nothing like this at home."

"Cereal and dry bread, I think, when we return to Richmond," Abigail smilingly groaned slightly.

"Anything planned for when we get back?" Poppy asked tentatively.

"We are working on a whole range of things – public appearances, book signings and such like," Abigail explained. "Nothing set in stone as yet. We will all probably need a week or two's rest and recouperation ready for the march through summer towards Christmas. You will also need to put pen to paper for the sequel. You do *want* to do a sequel … don't you?"

"Halfway through, my dear friend," Poppy returned with whooped satisfaction before dropping her hands jokingly to support her full belly, with an exaggerated groan.

"I knew you'd say that," Poppy's friend said, rubbing her hands in glee. "I love these events. Only one thing that we might change though."

"Grace?" came Poppy's tentative answer.

"We love to take her places and give her experiences we know she will enjoy, remember and cherish in later life," Abigail explained seriously. "However, she needs to spend more time at home with other youngsters, and being able to see her grandparents, whom she loves, much more often."

"I understand," Poppy agreed. "Although, I should have loved to have done half of what she has experienced even at her age."

"She's not far off school age now, either," Abigail added stoically. "That she attends school is a legal requirement, although it was not so in our day."

"Mine neither," Poppy said, vivid memories of school with George leaping into her mind. The shock registered on her teacher's face when she told her a few home truths, brought as much of a smile to her lips now as it had done then. Times had changed beyond all recognition, making her wonder how much they would alter in the future in this ever-changing and moving world. As a writer embracing such improvements, she welcomed the differences flashing around her, which sometimes made her feel giddy on her constant merry-go-round. Yet, how was she going to deal with seeing her Nanny Nell and Grandpa Ross?

"I've thoroughly enjoyed the sights and sounds of this wonderful city, Abigail, my dear friend," Poppy continued after a moment or two's reflection. "All down to the two of you … and Grace, of course."

"It has been our undoubted pleasure," her friend replied with a smile. "Don't forget that you have paid for it all, and for that we are very grateful. It has been excitingly lovely and has been something we would never have undertaken without you."

"The last couple of days too – after the book launch had flashed by – have been unbelievable," Poppy eulogised. "We never had time to see all of those places as tourists when we came on our Grand Tour. Mont Martre with the Sacre Coeur and its cafes surrounding it, the 'Iron Lady' Eiffel Tower. I loved the bouquinistes, with their second-hand book stalls along the banks of the River Seine. Breath-taking! Perhaps one day, **_Faithfully Yours_** will be on sale there."

"This railway station…?" Poppy puzzled at how busy it had become as they waited for the train to take them on to the Cote d'Azur on the shores of the Mediterranean Ocean. It was already eleven o'clock in the evening, and she – and Grace – were confused as to why so late.

"As you can see it is called 'Le Train Bleu' or Blue Train," Hal began to explain. "Purely and simply because the sleeping cars are gold and blue, of which there are—"

"Ten!" Grace whooped for joy. "I did counted them. Sleeping cars, Daddy? Does it mean they fall asleep as soon as we step through the doors? And … and … do we fall asleep as soon as we sit down?"

The three adults, and several around them, burst into fits of laughter at Grace's observations.

"No, my sweetie," Hal said patiently, with a grin and a guffaw. "It means that we go to sleep as soon as the train departs for the South of France."

"But," she pondered, a very puzzled expression growing. "I haven't brought my comfy bed. How will I sleep standing up?"

"There are very comfy beds in each sleeping compartment," her daddy replied patiently. "And *our* compartments we can lock so that no-one else can come in without we let them. We can also get something to eat whenever we like."

"Can we get something to eat now, please?" she uttered. "I am famished."

"That's a new one!" Poppy laughed. "My, doesn't she know some stuff!"

"Her daddy's favourite saying," Abigail explained with eyes glancing to the skies. "He's *always* famished, isn't he, Gracie?"

"He eats a lot and a lot of times," Grace agreed. "He's always famished, is my daddy. Am I famished, Mammy?"

"Only very rarely, my little petal," her mother answered as people started to board.

"It's now ten past eleven," Hal urged. "The train is due to set off at twenty to midnight, so we need to find our compartments so we can drop our—"

"Sweet cases!" Grace butted in, to everyone's mirth. "Then, we can stop being famished. Come on, Mammy and Daddy. Are you coming, too, Auntie Poppy?"

"You wouldn't want to go without me, would you Grace?" Poppy asked with a straight face. "With your little *suit*case?"

"No," she added sternly. "If you don't go, I don't go."

"I like these comfy beds," Grace went on as they entered their compartments. She sat on her bed, and immediately the excitement left her face and utter tiredness overcame her as her eyes closed and she dropped into a deep slumber.

The train hooted and pulled away from the platform slowly to start its nineteen-hour journey south. The Gare du Nord's impressive superstructure disappeared behind them as the Blue

Train slipped into the blackness, clickety-clacking over the track joints and points.

It was eleven forty-four, and Poppy felt a frisson of excitement coursing through her veins as thoughts of her Nanny Nell and Grandpa Ross stole into her sleepy mind.

The train clattered and juddered around Paris's 'Little Belt' rail line to pick up further passengers at the Gare de Lyon railway station before it gathered speed for its onward journey to the Mediterranean hot spots.

After the initial two or three hours, Poppy's sleep became fitful and disturbed, with elements of her recently very busy life as a popular author flashing in and out of her mind in jumbled, garish mixtures. The bulbous face of Peter Olleranshaw thrust itself at her, its tiny eyes disappearing into its ever-increasing mass.

In the early hours, the city of Dijon's geometrically patterned terracotta green, yellow and black roof grew out of the surrounding gloom, as the train slowed to a juddering halt both to herald breakfast time and to allow other passengers to climb aboard.

"Bit early to eat, don't you think?" Poppy suggested once they all had risen and dressed. Grace still slept soundly.

"Too early?" Hal muttered incredulously. "Indeed … not!! I'm—"

"Famished?" Abigail interrupted, to Poppy's titters. "I feel a little peckish myself. What time do we reach our destinations?"

"Lyon by around nine-ish, and Marseilles by about half past two this afternoon," he explained. "Nice by seven this evening."

"Plenty of time to stave off our hunger, then," Abigail uttered quietly.

"Good Lord, yes!" Hal responded urgently.

"I'm not hungry yet," Poppy chipped in. "So, you two nip off for your *first* early morning sustenance, and I'll sit here with Grace."

"You sure?" Abigail asked, checking that her friend wasn't just being polite.

"Quickly, then," Poppy replied with a smile, "before they run out of food, and Hal becomes ultra-famished."

Chapter 19

"I'm sorry, Old Chap," Jonas insisted. "Which part of 'No, I don't know what you are talking about' don't you understand? Have you heard of my disability that precludes me from *any* sort of physical activity?"

He knocked on his wooden leg, resulting in a dull thudding that raised a few eyebrows in the interview room.

"Where did you get enough money to allow you to live in the most expensive part of town, then?" an interviewing police sergeant asked rather pointedly.

"*That* I do not need – by law – to share with *you*," Jonas returned forcefully. "Suffice it to say that I have been very lucky in business."

"And that is?" the policeman asked again.

"Again, irrelevant," Jonas insisted. "It is enough to say that it was just before yon farmer's lad destroyed my leg with his giant hob-nailed boots and reduced me to … this. I won't ask you what this is all about, but I do need to speak to my solicitor, who will, no doubt, make everything straight."

"You can go now, Mr Jamieson," the policeman responded blandly. "If you have any information about the robbery at Thresher Hall in the future, please let us know."

"Would you be so good as to take me *back*, then, Old Chap," Jonas asked pointedly. "You know … home?"

"I'm afraid we have no available transport," the policeman retorted. "And there are no officers free to do so."

"May I borrow your telephone to arrange transport, then?" Jonas asked again with more than a little obvious frustration and anger, as he got to his feet with difficulty.

"If you'd like to make your way out, there is a *public* telephone in the outer office," the policeman suggested with a smirk.

~

"And why did they, stupid plods, drag you in in the first place?" Toby asked once he had helped his 'dad' from the Lanchester into the house.

"Harassment, my dear Toby," Jonas responded with a smirk. "They still hold their cherished belief that I will make a tragic slip and cough everything. They will have to wait a long time before that happens."

"I will always be around should you need me," Toby assured him. "They're not going to get one over on us."

"If we play them at their own game, we will always be several steps ahead of 'em," his stepdad returned with confidence. "Have no fear."

"I have a little 'errand' I should like you to perform while your mamma is sorting out our much-awaited repast," Jonas said quietly to his stepson in the study at the back of the house. "A little something that will be to our collective benefit."

"Nothing not … *straight forward*, I assume?" Toby asked carefully.

"Strictly kosher, I can assure you," Jonas said. "It's a little 'trinket' I should like you to take to Parsons' jeweller in town. Once Mr Parsons sees it he will know, and he will offer you a heavy brown envelope. Please bring it back to me. It will be well worth your while."

"I don't need paying, Pop," Toby complained mildly. "I—"

"Consider what I will give you … as a gift, father to son, for your birthday," Jonas said with a wink.

"But, it's not my birthday!" Toby went on.

"It will be … sometime this year," was his stepfather's swift reply.

"On my way … Father," Toby replied with a wink and a grin as he left the study.

"Not a word to your mamma, mind?" Jonas responded as he touched the side of his nose. "And don't be late for dinner."

Already eight o'clock on a dark and threateningly cold Saturday evening, George made his weary way into the kitchen. The occasional flash of lightening and distant rumble of thunder told him that a storm may be on its way. April was always a difficult month for him as its dour weather often drew him into inexplicable bouts of depression.

His daughter was already in bed, having been looked after for the whole day by his formed sister-in-law, Annabel. Although he was extremely tired after a thirteen-hour day, he still missed his little cherub, Alice, not to mention her mother. Once their names and faces sprang into his already overladen mind, a thick black cloud dragged his thoughts into an even darker place that he didn't seem able to escape.

He slid off his coat and boots and slumped into his favourite fire-side settee to stare into the red and yellow fingers trying to escape up the chimney back.

His neck bristled and his back stiffened as gently soft fingers stroked his skin, causing him to close his eyes, relax his shoulders and to sigh in ecstasy. His mind jumped back to the evenings he spent in such happiness with his wife, Alice, after many a hard day.

"George," a very familiar, soft voice oozed into his senses. "Lovely to be near you."

"Annabel?" he gasped. "You have no idea how good that feels. No! Don't stop. Please?"

He took hold of her hand tenderly and guided her body around the settee and on to his lap, where he brought her unresisting face towards his. Kissing her fully on her soft, warm lips, he drew her body next to his in a sensual embrace that both gloried in.

The only sound to be heard were the mutterings of his daughter's sleeping, the occasional creaking of Charity's bed springs, and the distantly detached grumbles of thunder as the storm veered north, away from their peace.

George awoke slowly into the pitch black of an unearthly early Sunday morning. He looked around trying to focus on anything familiar that might hint at where he was. Unusually for him he had neither woken nor even moved throughout a really deep and satisfying sleep where even his bed lay undisturbed.

Coming to terms with having to rise at some stage, Annabel's beautiful face drifted into his still uncertain mind. Although he could still feel the softness of her voluptuous lips on his and still had the scent of her hair in his nostrils, he was able to remember nothing between her sitting close to him on the settee and … now.

"Good morning, George," a very familiar voice greeted him as he shambled into the kitchen to prepare his breakfast. "Welcome to the land of the living."

"Annabel?" he mumbled as he shielded his eyes from the intrudingly bright sunlight. "What—?"

"Maisie and I are just about to have breakfast," she replied. "Will you be joining us?"

Maisie scrambled from her seat near the window, and with a joyful "Daddy!" she launched herself at him. He caught her in mid-flight and drew her little frame to him, hugging her and kissing her upturned face with joy.

"Will you have your turny-over eggs with us?" Maisie said eagerly. "And some toasty bread?"

"Whatever you're having is good enough for me," he answered happily. It had been a long while since he and his closest had shared even a modicum of family time together, and even though they hadn't been up long, he was beginning to enjoy what might be on offer. His daughter was beginning to regain herself which brought a bit of a sparkle back to George's eyes.

"Would you like to play a game with me, Daddy, after we've eaten?" Maisie asked, a look of anticipation on her little face.

"What had you in mind?" he requested, intrigued as to what games in these modern days might be different from those he played as a nipper with his older sisters. It didn't do to play with Mother and Father, because they weren't *real* players. *They* were parents, and parents didn't play with children's toys.

"Well," Maisie began to explain, "there's 'Snakes and Ladders' or 'Tiddly Winks' or … or … my favourite game is … 'Snap!'" she chuckled excitedly in anticipation that they might choose her bestest game.

"Would it be a good idea to wash up first and tidy away, do you think?" Annabel suggested. "And then count me in – if you would like me to play with you?"

"Of course we would," Maisie insisted, excitement building in her voice, "Daddy?"

"Sounds like a lot of fun," George agreed. "Why would we not want Annabel to play our games with us? My favourite of those is 'Snakes and Ladders' followed closely by … 'Snap!'"

He looked across at Annabel with satisfaction growing in his face, to be returned by her. She was pretty sure what she would like to happen – apart from work – after fun with this little girl and her dad.

⌒〜⌒

"What was in the package you gave me to hand over, Boss?" Toby inquired as he handed over a large, sturdy brown envelope to his stepfather.

"Any reason for your asking, Old Chap?" he replied.

"I just … wondered," the lad responded with a shrug.

"Just a small … trinket that he'd always fancied, and for which I had no further use," Jonas explained. "I'd had it for quite a few years and felt I might raise a few shillings by selling it to him."

"Did you get much for it?" Toby said, thinking *that* question might be one too far.

"Two hundred and fifty pounds," Jonas returned, almost in passing.

"Two…?" Toby gasped in shock as he bounced his backside into the settee. "But that's an amount of cash I never thought I would see, let alone handle."

"And this is for you," Jonas said, taking out of the package two large white five-pound notes and handing them to the lad.

"This is not a payment, but a gift to allow you to have money of your own. Take it or I'll give it to your mother."

Toby gasped again but accepted the gift, never having seen such an amount.

"Somebody mentioning my name?" Jenny offered with a smile as she entered the room. "Have you seen a ghost, Son? Your face seems to be utterly shocked."

"And this, my lovely wife, is for you," Jonas said, handing over the package her son had brought from the jeweller's.

"What's this?" she queried warily. "It feels quite heavy."

"Have a look inside," he urged. "With it I am suggesting also you take this bank book and deposit *that* amount into *your own* account, to be touched by you and *you* alone," Jonas urged. "That is a safeguard for the future in case anything happens to me."

Mouth agape and face bearing a stunned look, she flicked into the bank book, noticing one sole entry.

"But…!" she challenged. "That's a lot of money. What am I supposed to do with that amount? One thousand pounds? Where did it come from?"

"In case anything happens to me, you will have the where-withal to continue living here," Jonas answered quietly. "It came from wise investments I have made in your name, and that amount will grow steadily. It *is* legal and it is … yours. Northallerton Savings Bank."

"I don't know what to say," she reacted nonplussed and dumbfounded at his generosity.

Chapter 20

The excitement in the McIntyre cabin was electrifyingly palpable. Grace couldn't sit still for more than a few moments, even when she sat on her daddy's lap.

"Mammy, are we there yet? I can't see the Meddy Raininam Sea or any other sea for that matter," she grumbled lightly, shuffling from lap to window seat to carriage door. "Why are there so many people standing in the corridor next to us? Are they excited, too?"

Poppy loved this little scrap to bits, thinking that one day she might have liked a little one of her own with her George, but that was now a distant, fading dream. Why hadn't he been more organised and forthcoming when he had the opportunity? Why hadn't she been more forgiving and understanding when she ought to have been, avoiding the aggravation and upset caused to them both.

Grace's whoops of excited joy jolted Poppy from her deep, sad thoughts as the train ambled into this wonderful Cote d'Azur Railway Station that had been purposely set back from the sea front.

"We're here! We're here!" the little lassie shouted. "I can't see Granny and Grandpa Booth anywhere! Are they here? Will they—?"

"All right, my little one, time to calm down," Hal urged as he pulled her onto the seat between him and the window. "Patience will allow you to see better, and to cheer when the train comes to a halt in the railway station itself. All right?"

"Yes, Daddy," she responded quietly, but with quietly jiggling legs whose feet also sought to find the carriage floor. "Will you please tell me when we are there and then we can chair together? You will chair *with* me, won't you?"

"*Cheer*, my sweetie, *cheer*," Abigail corrected her daughter with a slightly supressed smile. "We'll *all cheer*, shall we?"

"Yes!" Grace re-emphasised. "All of us!"

As the train slowed along the platform, the glorious architecture, influenced from the Louis XIII era of the sixteen hundreds, its Arles stone sculptures, forged steel roof and grand chandeliers urged a sense of awe. Although the train's movement forwards seemed to continue, its stop urged Grace to begin a muted cheer which was joined by Hal, Abigail *and* Poppy, who now had developed a feeling of feared anticipation ahead of the meeting with Nanny Nell and Grandpa Ross.

"Mammy! Daddy!" Grace uttered as they disembarked from their home of the last twenty-four hours. "Look! Is that yooj round thing up there a *real* clock?"

"That huge thing is most definitely a real clock," Abigail announced. "If you look closely for a minute or two, you will see its big hand moving."

"I see! I see!" Grace replied after a minute or two's staring unblinking at the clock, her voice dropping almost to a whisper.

"All right then," Hal butted in having found a largish

trolley upon which to load all their suitcases ready to seek transport to Nanny and Grandpa's abode, where they would all part company. Once their luggage had been loaded, they made to move off to the outside of the station. After five or so paces, Abigail turned around to see why Poppy wasn't with them.

"Pop—!" she began, to be stopped by Hal's hand on her arm and his other hand pointing behind and off to the right. Poppy was moving off from them increasingly quickly to embrace…

"Nanny Nell! Grandpa Ross!" she cried, tears coursing down her cheeks, as she flung herself into her grandma and grandpa's arms. "I didn't expect—"

～

"We couldn't let you struggle to find us," Ross Senior explained. "So, knowing that the Train Bleu is almost always on time – to within five minutes or so – we came to you."

"But that large – very large – motor car?" Poppy gasped.

"We've had it for quite some time," Ross replied. "It helps with our weekly shopping."

They all laughed until Abigail and Hal finished their cups of tea and made to leave, grace asleep in her daddy's arms.

"We must away to our hotel and put this little one to her slumbers," Abigail told them.

"But we thought you would be staying here with us?" Ross said. "You have your own suite of two rooms, a bathroom and a kitchen/dining area. You can come and go as you please or spend as much time with us as you would wish."

"I don't know what to say," Hal responded in shock.

"Your magic words would perhaps begin with … Yes," Ross laughed. "Don't forget that we haven't see any of you for an eternity, and we would rather like to hear all your news – first hand – about what you have been up to, particularly with reference to our granddaughter's success at writing romance stories. What do you say?"

"Then our magic response would undoubtedly be … 'Yes please'," Abigail responded. "We would be delighted to take up your wonderfully generous offer."

"I have someone I'd like you to meet, Poppy, a little later on today," Grandpa Ross suggested over morning coffee the day after they had settled into their new luxurious life style along the Promenade des Anglais, overlooking the Mediterranean Ocean.

"Prospective husband?" Poppy asked, a mischievous look playing around her eyes. "Do you know, Grandpa Ross, that this balcony is larger than the whole ground floor of my cottage? Of course you do. You are the one that engineered its conversion from a derelict box."

"Seriously, my dear, he is married to the richest lady around, and they have houses – retreats they call them – in several European countries," he retorted. "He is American, and she is – I've no idea, really. His name is Garry Smithson.

"He is almost twice your age," Ross added after a moment's thought. "He's also a leading light in … publishing and the promotion of up-and-coming young writers' work."

"Why is he interested in me, Grandpa?" Poppy puzzled. "I've only done three signings – really only two outside my home area."

"Don't look so puzzled, because he's heard of you and thinks you would go down a well in … the U S of A."

Poppy sat there with mouth open and eyes aghast, only able to say, "Heard of *me*? Was that from you, by any chance?"

"No, really," he assured her. "He has literary contacts in London and Paris who notified him of this young English author called Poppy Spence. His Paris contact is called Giles Garibaldi and—"

"That's the name of the owner of the bookshop in Paris!" she said, startled beyond belief.

"Well then, small world, eh?" Ross returned. "Garry believes you would 'go down a storm' – American for 'do well', I believe."

⁓

"Mr Booth? Mr Ross Booth?" the young lady said nervously as a large man opened the door.

"Indeed, I am, miss," the man replied. "And to what do I owe the pleasure of meeting such a charming young lady as yourself?"

"May I come in, please? It's a little … chilly out here," she said.

"You are not from this part of the world, are you?" he said, placing a mug of steaming tea close to her on the small occasional table she was sitting next to by the fire.

"How did you guess that?" she asked with a puzzled frown.

"If you had been reasonably local, you wouldn't have been so flimsily dressed," he explained.

"But it's getting on for summer, isn't it?" she answered, non-too sure what he was meaning.

"Makes no difference what season you happen to find yourself in," Ross went on. "You always have to be prepared for the worst in this part of the world.

"Now, what can I do for you?" he asked after a moment or two, during which time his wife joined them from the kitchen. "May I introduce my wife, Martha?"

The young woman cleared her throat, clearly nervously embarrassed with what she was about to say.

"The Antipodes is it, perhaps?" he suggested.

"Sorry?" she said, not understanding what he was saying.

"Is it Australia you're from?" Ross went on.

"How did you know?" she asked, giggling nervously.

"Your accent is very different from ours, say?" Martha chipped in.

"Anyway, as we don't know you and you really have no idea who we are, why *are* you here?" Ross challenged.

"If you are Mr Ross Booth, I believe I'm your … daughter," she blurted out unceremoniously.

Husband and wife stabbed incredulous looks at each other at hearing this unusual statement, until Ross burst into peals of laughter, to be joined by his wife.

"Why do you laugh?" the young lady urged, nonplussed and embarrassed, with her face turning a deep shade of pink. "I know you are my father, and I have proof."

"Is this the first time either you or your mother have been to this country?" Martha asked once the laughter had settled.

"Yes, it is," the youngster muttered. "Why?"

"Well, my husband has never been to Australia," Martha returned sharply. "In fact, he has never been out of this country."

The young lady plumped back into her chair, a look of abject disappointment growing in her face.

"But that's im—!" she blurted out again.

"Possible?" Martha responded.

"Actually, that's strictly not true," Ross quickly butted in, to his wife's surprise and look of concern.

"Ross?" Martha said, turning to her husband, consternation growing.

"I stepped across the border, a few years ago, into … Scotland," he admitted with a grimace. "Never meant to but—"

"Ignore him, Miss…" Martha scoffed. "What is your name?"

"Booth," she replied. "Rosie Booth."

"Now then," Ross muttered. "My father is called … Ross Booth, and he spent a significant part of his life in Australia. You see, I'm not old enough to have a daughter of your age, and it would have been something of an immaculate conception if I had been anywhere near when you were conceived."

"Would it be possible to see your father, then?" Rosie answered. "Perhaps…"

"Certainly," he said, "but you would need to travel to the South of France, as that is where he now resides."

"South of France?" Rosie asked in surprise. "Why there?"

"Problems with his lungs from working too long with—" Ross began to explain.

"Sheep, by any chance?" the youngster suggested, causing Ross to stop abruptly what he was about to say. "My mother and father had a sheep farm until my father died from just such a disease. Our next-door neighbour helped us quite a lot until my mother also passed away, forcing me, as a youngster, to be looked after by my aunt Jeanie. She was the one that told me Ross Booth was my father.

⌒⌒⌒

"New York would be a fantastic place to float your novel," the man said. "I've read it and I couldn't put it down, even though romances are not my thing. There are millions of New Yorkers – and Americans in general – that are into romances in a big way."

"But how would I get there, Mr Smithson?" Poppy asked, not really following his reasoning. "I don't have wings and there is a lot of water between there and my home in England."

"Just do what the thousands of others have done from all over Europe over the years," he answered simply. "Take a boat – a big boat."

"The difficulty is that I need my management team with me and they have … family to consider," she returned.

"Take them with you," he said with a shrug of his ample shoulders.

"A big boat?" Poppy queried. "What do you mean by a … big boat?"

"Something like S.S.Titan?" he responded. "Now, that's a *very, very* big boat. It probably takes two thousand people in varying states of comfort. It's not cheap, mind you, but it can be very comfortable and luxurious, if you can afford it. Probably takes around six or seven days to cross to New York, but that's an experience in itself."

Poppy fell quiet for a little while, deep in thought when, suddenly, she turned to Abigail and Hal.

"What do you think, my dear friends?" Poppy asked, honestly needing their opinion, from which response she would make up her mind. "I will be guided by what you think."

Abigail and Hal looked at each other, the one raising a near invisible questioning eyebrow and the other delivering an almost imperceptible nod in response.

"We think it's a brilliant idea and we would love … to be included," she responded with a smile. "Don't worry about Grace. She will love it, too."

"What have we just done?" Poppy said with a slightly embarrassed giggle.

"You've only gone and done what any right-thinking and ambitious up-and-coming author would give her eyelids to do," Nanny Nell said, as she turned to her husband.

"I've heard of these liners," Ross said quietly. "Been sailing the Southampton to New York run since the latish eighteen hundreds. You have to be careful, though, as the more you pay the more you get. The corollary to that has to be avoided at all costs – if you'll pardon the pun. I believe this boat – the Titan? – is one of the biggest floating the oceans."

"Abigail and Hal will take care of all of that," Poppy joined in. "I trust them implicitly."

"How are your finances holding up with all this traipsing about?" Poppy's grandpa asked quietly. "Managing?"

"What with all the money you have invested in me, and my three huge book launches, I think you will be taking a return on your investment before long," she assured him.

"I want nothing in return, my dear Poppy," he returned firmly. "You need all you have, and, besides, we certainly don't need it. Have you seen where and how we live?"

"I'll look after you both in your old age, Grandpa Ross," Poppy chortled mischievously. "Don't you worry yourself."

Her grandparents burst into peals of good-humoured laughter at her sharp wit. Ross had enjoyed their company hugely and would be sorry to see them go. However, he couldn't let them go without having a quiet word with Hal concerning the money and contacts he proposed to leave to Poppy upon his death, which he would divulge to Hal at a later time.

Chapter 21

"Our home certainly feels empty and quiet since our dear Poppy and her friends departed," Nell said as they sat quietly on their large balcony overlooking the Mediterranean Ocean, drinking early afternoon tea and nibbling some of Nell's famous fruit cake that she made year-round. "That little treasure, Grace, is so smart and funny that it leaves me wondering if ever our granddaughter might see fit to present us with something similar."

"Not sure if that will ever happen," her husband replied. "We have to support her in her wishes to be as good as she can be in her chosen field. That, most definitely, is our overriding goal."

"Looking back all those years after her birth, I can't believe how single-minded she has become," Nell added. "Even from a very early age she was pert and knew what she wanted. I remember with fondness from her being six, at Christmas time, Ross taking her out into the fields to collect holly and ivy and what she called 'middletoe'. She was adamant that Christmas at Boulders Wood couldn't go ahead without her input. She even took it upon herself to welcome all the guests personally as they drew up to the front door."

"How I wish I'd been there!" Ross muttered quietly. "We have missed such a lot, you and I. And now, here we are, almost with a death sentence hanging over our head."

"No need to be so melancholic or melodramatic, my lovely man," Nell responded, her arm around his shoulders to reassure him. "As long as we take care and don't attempt anything too risky, we'll be together until eternity. What time are they likely to get home, by the way?"

"The evening Train Bleu sleeper was due to leave Nice last evening at eight o'clock, arriving at Paris Nord by twenty past two this afternoon," Ross explained. "The crossing from Calais to Dover would see them reaching London Victoria by around quarter to eleven this evening. Time for a hotel overnight stay, which they had already booked, ready for heading North tomorrow. All booked in advance, of course.

"That reminds me," he said after a few minutes of quiet contemplation. "I received a letter from our Ross this morning to say that a young lady called, looking for a 'Ross Booth'."

"And?" she queried.

"It turns out it wasn't him she was after," he went on.

"Past misdemeanours, perhaps, catching up with you?" Nell re-joined with a giggle.

"Well," he continued, "it seems like she was looking for her father who happened to be called … Ross Booth."

"Oh?" she puzzled. "What's that supposed to imply?"

"She is called Rosie; Rosie Booth," he said slowly. "That has to have some implications … somewhere. He has suggested that she is staying local to them, and perhaps we ought to return at some time in the near future to—"

"Sort things out?" Nell suggested. "She could be *anyone* trying it on."

"The strange thing is that she is Australian, and her parents were my neighbours on the adjoining sheep farm," Ross replied carefully but with conviction. "I remember them well. The chap died from the same condition I have. We need to go, Nell. We Need to—"

"No problems then," she interrupted sharply. "We'll do it in the next week or two?"

"All right," he agreed. "I don't know how long I've got, and I really need to see my son and his family before too long. I'll get on with the booking pretty soon."

"Did you have an affair with this girl's mother?" Nell asked quietly after a little while, not wishing to seem as if she was pushing him.

"Couldn't actually call it an affair when her husband had already died, leaving her with no local family, and my wife had passed away because of her predilection for alcohol," Ross explained without emotion. "We slept together once and once only. Within a week, she had gone, I assumed to stay with her sister in Sidney. I heard nothing further about or from her … until now, that is. Story of my life really, I suppose, until I met you again. *That* brought me back to life big style!"

"More tea and—?" Nell asked.

"Cake? Too right!" Ross butted in rapidly. "You know it's my favourite."

⌒

"It's an infection, Mr Jamieson," the doctor at the hospital offered. "It's one that needs urgent attention."

"Don't tell me you want to take away my remaining stump, Old Chap!" Jonas replied. "Can't I pay to have someone more senior to sort it out much more quickly than before?"

"You already are!" the doctor snorted. "I am the most senior surgeon here."

"Then what are you waiting for?" Jonas snorted. "Whatever it costs, please get rid of this excruciating pain."

"We have three remedies," the medic observed carefully. "Morphine is our number one, followed by heroine and laudanum. However, I have to be honest in that the first two can tend to be – how shall I put it? – habit-forming. If you take them for too long, they can become too difficult to rationalise."

"Rationalise?" Jonas asked, wincing from the insistently stabbing bouts of discomfort to his remaining stump. "What the hell does that mean?"

"You would find it very difficult to rid yourself of the craving for … more of the stuff, eventually turning you into an addict," the surgeon offered.

"And the other one – laudanum?" the patient questioned, desperate for an answer.

"Same, but not as efficient or quite as bad," the surgeon reacted. "Eventually it would lead to a similar addiction. I can take the pain away, but it doesn't last forever. The relief would only last so long. We have no cure for that sort of diseased tissue, and *that* would finish you off before release from the addiction."

"What are you saying, then?" the young man urged, expecting the worst.

"That we may have to 'trim' the remains of your leg stump to see if we might take away the poisonous disease," the doctor said with a shrug.

"By trim, you mean?" Jonas asked slowly, thinking that he might know what was coming next.

"Reducing it by half, which would trim it back to mid-thigh," he explained. "Difficult and not without pain, but it would be the only solution."

The hate he felt for that insidious wastrel, George Garside, began to grow until he thought he might explode what with what he felt against him for causing such agony and distress. If he were to survive the next bout of surgery, he would find George Garside and he would kill him!

⌐∾⌐

"I'm not sure I could go along with this idea of travelling half-way across the world to this … New York place," Poppy said to Abigail as they approached Paris on the Train Bleu. "Our home launch, London *and* Paris were invigoratingly exciting, but New York is not … here. It sounds it might be somewhat different from the original in Yorkshire."

"The original York was a Roman town called Eboracum in the first century," Hal chipped in, "and a very important one, too, as it was surrounded by a fortified wall with gates to allow ingress and exit."

"Trust Hal to have such knowledge whirling around in his head," Abigail said with a quick glance to the heavens.

"I find it amazing that he has," Poppy eulogised. "I wish I had a quarter as much in *my* head."

"All wonderful, but completely valueless," he offered without fear of contradiction. "I know several people that have visited this 'New' Eboracum, but have found it extremely busy, quite crowded and more than a little … dangerous to be alone in."

"Hal!" Abigail warned, nodding towards Poppy.

"She won't *be* alone," Hal emphasised. "She will have us and, apparently there will be some New Yorkers who work for and with Garry Smithson to make sure she gets the most out of this – short – visit. The only problem is that it will involve a lot of sailing about on water – around twelve to fourteen days between Southampton and New York. We will have to see if it will be worthwhile to spend three- or four-days book launching and signing."

"*Is* it going to be worth –?" Abigail asked with a grimace.

"While?" Hal Butted in. "Garry seems to believe there will be thousands of people that love reading *new* books, and *that* could boost Poppy's popularity significantly even more than London and Paris combined."

"Gracious me!" Poppy uttered, having listened closely to every word. "Would it be wise to bring Grace with us there? I mean—"

"Bearing the possible dangers in mind, probably not," Hal replied, concerned about his daughter's welfare even on an ordinary stroll down the main street from their home in the North Riding. "It might be as well to let her stay with your mother. Abigail?"

"Don't know," she said. "We might have to wait and see. When are we thinking of making this trip?"

"We have to return home, assess what Poppy's financial state is now, after all, the books so far sold have to be replaced," Hal observed with some degree of certainty. "This is possibly an opportunity that will be too good to turn down. We will have to be led to a certain extent by Garry Smithson and his company. After all, he knows North America better than we do."

"Daddy?" Little Grace piped in. "Are you as famished as I am? Because I think it has been a very long time since I last had something to eat and drink. In fact, I am more famisheder than ever before!"

The adults laughed at her expressions and the earnest look on her little face.

"I think we had better seek out somewhere they provide lots of famish-stopping food so our little girl doesn't collapse from hunger," Hal observed, picking up his daughter to seek out the diner, throwing her into the air to catch her again before they reached the door. Grace screamed in excitement and joy as he caught her.

"My uncle Ross used to do that with me when I was six," Poppy reminisced, memory drawing back those carefree but exciting times in her early years. It also drew back those frightening events around the time Grandpa Joss met his end … on the points of a Nanny Nell wielded pitchfork.

Chapter 22

"I'm very glad I brought my outdoor coat," Nell muttered as she shivered slightly on the platform. "This must be the only occasion I've agreed to wait on a draughty railway station platform to catch a train that will take us away from our gloriously clement climate. Are you sure you *want* to traipse all the way back to the North Riding … at this time?"

"This is the *usual* time for the Train Bleu to start its journey back to Calais, ready for the ferry across to England," Ross explained … again.

"Tell me again," she asked. "How long do we have to wait on this draughty cold station platform for the train that is called Blue. Why is it called the Blue Train, pray?"

"Because its sleeper carriages are *painted* blue, as you can see, because here it comes now," he laughed drawing his wife to him for a bit of warmth. "It is due to set off for Paris's Nord station at precisely eight pm, and it is now seven fifty. Just ten minutes to find and board our overnight sleeper before it departs."

Pleased to escape from an unusually chilly evening, they found their berth very quickly and closed its door on the outside world.

"Good gracious!" Nell gasped as they sat down. "How lovely is this! Never done anything like this before."

"Me neither," Ross agreed. "It's like being in a First-Class hotel – seats, bed, bed covers – absolutely wonderful. I think we've made the right decision to leave now."

"Right decision? How do you mean?" Nell asked, puzzled at his reference. "You're not thinking about going back … to England, are you? To stay?"

"No, but we are going at the appropriate time," he returned carefully. "Remember the slight chill outside, and the inordinate breeze?"

"And?" she replied, still not knowing where the conversation was leading.

"It's all the effect of the strange wind that the locals call 'Le Mistral'," Ross began to explain. "There are lots of mountains in and around this country – Alps, Pyrenees, the Vosges – that can funnel the wind towards and even across the Cote d'Azur, depending on the time of year. The coldest period because of this can be between November and April."

"So, it all depends on—" Nell offered.

"When during the year it blows," he said. "Making it last a day or two, or even several weeks. I'm not a weather guesser, but I'm glad not to be here for the next week or two. Temperature might tumble as low as fifty-five- or sixty-degrees Fahrenheit."

"That's not cold! Is it?" she muttered with a frown.

"Definitely not, but the strength of The Mistral is governed by weather conditions – gentle breeze to gale force," Ross declared. "It will be much colder in our neck of the woods.

Don't forget."

Nell leaned back into the plushiness of her easy chair, sipping a glass of sparkling Champagne slowly as it tended to cause her to sneeze if she drank it too quickly.

"Time for something to eat?" she suggested. "Feels like an age since we ate last. When do we stop again?"

"Quite a number along the Cote d'Azur – Cannes, Antibes, Juan-les-Pins, Saint-Raphael – all briefly to pick up more passengers. The next major stop will be Marseilles at half past midnight, Lyon at just after six in the morning and Paris at twenty past two tomorrow afternoon," he replied.

"Gracious! I am really glad to have you with me," Nell chuckled, quite overwhelmed at how important he had become to her. "I wouldn't be able to remember all of that."

"It comes with spending so many years counting sheep!" he retorted with a snigger. "You will no doubt have noticed that I never have any trouble with getting off to sleep either."

~

Joseph awoke suddenly with a start, knowing full well that the vivid dream he had just been thrust out of was nowhere close to reality. He was hot, sweaty and uncomfortable even though the sheets from his side of the bed were almost all on the floor. What was *that* all about? Where had those sometimes-erotic dreams come from? And who was … Livia? No-one he had ever met. So, why—?"

"You all right? Lilly Victoria asked quietly turning towards him. "Joseph?"

"Very disturbing dreams," he muttered as she reached out to touch him gently. Throughout his explanation and close detail, she made neither comment nor gave any sign that she was affected by what he had told her.

"Do you remember when the girls and I left you for a short time, a year or two ago?" she reminded him.

"Vaguely, yes," he replied. "But that's quite a long time ago."

"True," she answered. "But not so long ago that I can't remember in great detail the dreams that hit me hard when I was on my own, without you."

"I don't understand the relevance of that to what I have just experienced," Joseph responded carefully.

"My dreams were very … similar to what you have just described," she went on to explain. "I hadn't slept with you or … *been* with you for weeks on end."

"But you—?" Joseph answered, still puzzled by what she had to say.

"How long is it since we … made love … together?" she asked pointedly. "You know, actually did—"

"I understand what you are saying," he responded with a quizzical frown. "But what—?"

"The body sometimes plays funny tricks on the mind … and vice versa," she started to explain. "We haven't made love … had sex … whatever you want to call it … for several weeks."

"I've been very busy," he said defensively. "And there's been the children. We don't…"

"They are now of school age," she replied deliberately slowly. "You could make time during the day so that we could spend some time … together."

"What has this got to do with—?" he said, more puzzled than ever.

Finally, his brain began to understand what she was saying. She was right! How could he not have seen that before? Livia? Lilly Victoria!

"This is not the first time it has happened recently either," he muttered softly, drawing her naked body to his. "I even thought—"

"That I wasn't bothered?" she butted in with a demure smile. "*That* couldn't be further from the truth. All you had – have – to do is … talk to me, and you would be in no doubt whether – when – I want *you*."

"Like—?" he started.

"Now?" she said with a quiet giggle, snuggling up to him.

~

"Not seen our Poppy for quite a while," Ross said over mid-morning tea and snack of a generous doorstopper of a cheese sandwich.

"She called in the other day when you were in Northallerton, along with Abigail and her nipper, Grace," Joseph responded. "It sounds like she has had a dramatically interesting last few weeks, what with book launches in London and Paris, and even their trip to Southern France to see your father and our mam. That must have been something else!"

"I heard about that only briefly," Ross returned. "I need to sit down with her and get chapter and verse about what's going on."

They were interrupted by a heavy knocking on the door.

"Wonder what's so urgent?" Ross puzzled as he strode to the door to see who needed entry at this time of day.

"Father! Mother! Poppy!" he gasped as he hugged all three. "I wasn't expecting this! Don't just stand there! Come in and I'll get Mary-Jane to prepare you some—"

The kitchen door clicked open as Mary-Jane carried a tray full of cups, tea pot, plates and cakes into the room. She placed it on the large table in front of the crackling fire, and made to leave.

"Please stay with us, Mary-Jane," Poppy suggested. "There is something I would like to share with you, too."

"Just look at that spread!" Ross Senior drooled. "I knew there was a reason why we came back from the warm Mediterranean to the startlingly chilly North Riding!"

As they settled around the table for a mite to eat and drink, another rattle at the outside door urged Ross Junior to stride to the door again.

"Hello again," he greeted the newcomer quietly. "Do come in. Just in time for a cup of tea and a bite of the most gorgeous cake.

"Father, I should like you to meet this young lady," Ross said as he escorted the young lady to the table to seat her opposite his father. "Her name is … Rosie Booth, and she believes you are her … father."

The room fell silent while all those around the table cast looks at one another, unsure what to make of Ross's bald statement.

"Rosie, is it?" Ross Senior's voice cut gently into the overwhelming silence.

"Indeed, it is," the young lady replied.

"How is your mother?" Ross asked again.

"No longer with us, I'm afraid," Rosie said quietly. "She died when I was twelve. She had told me about my father, and I have spent the last years looking for … you."

"Why did you want to find him now?" Nell asked cynically. "Money?"

Gasps from the audience made Nell realise that *that*, perhaps, was not the question to ask, shown on Ross Senior's face as he turned to look at his wife.

"Actually, no," Rosie replied. "Two or three reasons, really. It turns out that my mother was quite well off because she had sold the farm just before we left and made quite a large amount of money out of it, which I inherited. I need to find my dad, because I have no other family, and I don't like being alone. Lastly, realising that my mother and her husband – who was not my father – died from the same illness, I wanted to find my father to warn him of the costs of spending most of his life with sheep."

"Then, as everything falls into place, I can't be anything other than … your father," Ross Senior said as he put his arms around his daughter.

"At last!" Rosie sighed as she hugged her father at last. "Alone no more."

"Do you realise, Rosie, that now you have not only found your father, but you have also gained a brother," Ross Junior informed her as he picked her up, feet not touching the floor in a heart-felt hug. "We are now your only family, and very pleased we are to receive you to our midst."

"Have you anywhere to live?" Rosie's father asked, concerned that she might have to stay at a local hostelry, some of which were not the most salubrious.

"I'm staying at the Grand in Richmond," she returned. "Is that all right?"

"Good hotel, but you would be better placed among your own," her new brother butted in.

"How do you mean? I don't understand…" Rosie replied somewhat nonplussed at the expression.

"He's a Yorkshireman, Rosie," Nell interjected with a smile. "He means you should be staying with your own family. I believe he is offering you a place here—"

"For as long as you need it," he interrupted.

"Take no notice of him," Martha commented. "It's good to meet a new member of our exclusive clan, and I'll show you where you can stay in a little while."

"Your kindness is so overwhelming," Rosie said quietly, tears gathering. "I am so glad I have found you all when all I wanted was to meet my real father. And now I have a whole real family with whom to enjoy the rest of my life."

"What about your 'stuff' in Australia?" Ross Junior asked. "Don't you want to make sure it joins you over here?"

"The only 'stuff' I have is what I am standing up in, and what is in my baggage," Rosie pointed out. "Once settled, I can buy whatever property is available within access to you all."

CHAPTER 23

"But I don't see how feasible what you suggest is going to be," Mary-Jane said to her Aunt Mary, sitting over lunch in the back room of Mary's Pantry.

"How do you mean, lass?" Mary answered, not sure where this was going.

"If you take over the property next door to expand Mary's Pantry and put me in charge, you will add extra costs," she said. "Wouldn't that make you less profitable?"

"All well and good if we maintain the same menu throughout," Mary explained. "However, I want *you* to provide something of equally high quality, but also a menu that is quite … different. Something that will support and complement what *we* do in here. Are you with me?"

"I understand fully and am very much with you!" Mary-Jane assured her, rubbing her hands together eagerly, and wearing a glint in her eyes. "I'll put a few ideas together for what we might offer as an enhancement of what you do here."

"'Ang on a bit!" her Uncle Geoffrey urged in his best North Riding accent. "We 'aven't even begun to pursue enquiries yet!"

"I have spoken to Doreen Parker who owns the shop next door, and *she* says they will be retiring very soon this year," Mary said, making him entertain little doubt that things *would* go ahead as they had planned. "Also, I've already been elevated to the top of the ladder – several rungs above anyone else, I'll have you know, Geoffrey – ready to hand over the lease."

"Ah, but—" Geoffrey tried to have his say, knowing full well that *his* ideas would always be ignored … politely.

"No 'ah buts', my lovely husband," she countered firmly, casting her definite nod in her niece's direction. "We *will* be moving forward on this one before Mary-Jane moves else-where. There is nobody as good as her in the baking field."

"'Ere, Missis!" a deeply gruff voice accosted Mary. "This 'ere little bugger has been trying to steal your pies from the counter at t'front on t'café. I'll nip round for a copper to tek 'im down to t'police station."

"No, don't do that, Mr Stubbs," Mary urged. "Leave him with me, if you please."

"All rayt," the man with the gruff voice returned as he turned to go. "And thee young 'un, I know who thy is, so stay thiyer."

"Jimmy?" Mary said, pulling her spectacles down from her forehead. "Jimmy Brown? What's to do, Jimmy?"

"I'm sorry, Missis," he replied quietly, his eyes fixed on his almost soleless boots.

"Come on," she urged. "Tell me. What's up?"

"Mi mam and mi sister 'ave 'ad nowt to eat for two days," he started. "So, I thought you wouldn't miss a piece o' bread."

"And how long has it been since you had anything to eat, eh?" Come on now!" Mary asked quietly. "More than a couple of days, I should think."

"Come here," she urged him, holding out her hand towards him. He hesitated; not sure what she would do. He had seen many an adult hand held out to him and felt their hardness across his face and head.

"Come on," she insisted. "Nobody's going to hurt you."

"Three days," he admitted, with downcast face. "I don't feel too well."

"Come through into the back of the shop," she offered. "There you will have your fill of what you would like to eat and drink, and—"

He covered his face with his open hands, and his sobs interrupted what she was about to say. His little shoulders shook until she thought he would collapse onto the floor. She drew him to her to let him know that everything was going to be all right.

"When you have finished your tea, I am going to take you and this bag of food to keep you and your family going for a few days," Mary promised him. "When that's run out, I will bring you some more. Is that all right? Will your mam be all right with that?"

"Yes … she … will," the little lad croaked, his words finding it hard to steer around his heart-felt sobs.

"Come on then," she went on. "Over here and let's see you tucking in. I don't want to see any of this food left. It's all good stuff that I'm sure you will love."

"Thank you, Missis," Jimmy said, trying to make sure he didn't gobble. "This is … lovely."

"It's not far from closing, so we'll take you home when you've finished your tea," Mary explained. "Your mam and your sister can have some of the same."

"You do know your way home, I trust?" she went on after a moment or two's breather from trying to push as much down his throat as he was able.

"Yes, Missis," he answered. "It's just round t'next corner, down towards t'river. I don't know what else to say."

"Then don't say anything," she advised him. "How old is your sister?"

"She's fifteen I think," Jimmy returned slowly. "I'm not sure."

"Does she go to school?" Mary asked.

"Don't think so," he said. "But neither do I. Never have done. Mi Mam can't afford it. *She* says she hoped I will soon be able to earn some money."

"What does your mam do?" Mary went on. "Does *she* work?"

"She can't," Jimmy responded reluctantly. "She can't walk very well because mi dad broke her leg when he came home one night after he had filled his belly wi' so much ale, he could barely walk hissen."

"Broke her leg?" May gasped. "How? Why?"

"He landed out wi' 'is boot across her knee, and she went down screaming in pain," he continued, "and it's bin t'same ever since."

"Has she seen a doctor?" Mary asked. "Or been to the hospital?"

"We can't afford to," he said. "No money."

"We'll see about that," Mary commented firmly as she and her husband readied themselves to visit Jimmy Brown's mam.

A heavy banging at the door awoke George from his introverted reverie in the gloom of his front room where a glowing fire cast eerie shadows. Why was it somebody allus had to disturb him from his rest when he had only just settled in his favourite easy chair by the chimney breast? This was where he always settled after his evening meal, rarely retiring to bed before midnight.

"Yes?" he growled a little irritably as he opened the door, bending down to pick up a piece of paper that had just dropped, he was shocked back to the here and now by a fist grazing the top of his head. He jerked upright very quickly to catch some strange attacker under the chin with the top of his head. This catapulted his assailant backwards, stunned, allowing George to regroup and deliver a crunching blow to the head with his loose-laced boot. The assailant collapsed in a heap, unconscious, blood oozing from the side of his face.

Rummaging in a sideboard drawer, George retrieved a couple of pieces of sturdy rope, each long enough to bind securely both hands and feet.

"What's all the noise?" George's sister's voice joined him from the foot of the stairs, to be followed by Annabel. They both gasped when they caught sight of the intruder in the doorway.

"Who's this, and why is he unconscious *and* bleeding *and* tied up in the doorway?" Florence asked. "Is he still breathing?"

"Hopefully not," George said, explaining what had happened as he finished tying up the miscreant.

It was at this time they heard the unmistakeable sound of some-one hot-footing it across the gravelly courtyard to the side of the house.

"Two attackers, then?" Florence observed. "But who and why?"

"I think we can hazard a realistic guess, don't you?" George said with a more than murderous look in his eyes.

His two companions shrugged and shook heads, not understanding what he was asking.

"Well, who is usually behind anything that happens to me?" he returned sharply. "No idea?"

Both heads shook dismissively.

"It's obvious my arch enemy, Jonas Jamieson, is behind this, and always has been," he reiterated, his venom surprising his audience.

"Don't you think you are being a bit paranoid?" Florence butted in, much to his annoyance.

"Recall the knife in my back? No? Well, I do," he spat out aggressively. "I can feel it as if it's still there – everyday. It's him. I know it is."

"But don't you remember what you inflicted upon him?" she pointed out again. "I believe he has only one leg, following on from the literal kicking you dished out to him. Don't you think you ought to call it quits by now?"

"What just happened to me, Florence?" George answered, more than a little angered by her answers, gainsaying what he, the head of the family, was pointing out so obviously.

"It could have been anybody, Brother," she replied. "Anybody that wanted to try to make a fast shilling. What's the paper in your hand, by the way?"

"This lump here must have dropped it as I came to the door," George explained as he handed it over to his sister. "Actually, it saved me, because I bent down to pick it up just before I felt the wind of his fist through my hair."

"It says 'I told you so!'" Florence read, a puzzled look developing in her face. "What does that mean?"

"Most definitely him," George reiterated. "He always leaves a note to remind me that, even in his lame state, he has me by the throat."

Florence was stunned. Perhaps her brother was right…

"Cup of tea, anyone?" Annabel broke the gathering silence.

Chapter 24

"In a week's time, we will be returning to The South of France," Ross Senior announced over afternoon tea in the sitting room.

"South of France?" Rosie remarked, stunned that she would be losing him again. "But why when your family is here?"

"Do you remember one of the reasons you wanted to find me?" he returned. "The one about your parents and the sheep?"

"Indeed, I do," she agreed. "And I am glad that I did. Why?"

"Well, the same thing is happening to me," he explained. "That is why we live in Nice – doctor's sage advice."

Rosie fell silent, shocked by his revelation. Was the nightmare that she shared with her mother about to revisit her again – with her true father this time?

"We live in a lovely area just about on the shoreline of the Mediterranean Ocean," he went on, noticing her obvious distress. "The climate is rather more conducive to having a year-round comfortable existence, too."

"Expensive, but lovely," Nell added. "Could be somewhere for you to settle down, my dear. Such a lot to do and people to meet."

"But, what about the rest of the family?" Rosie asked, not sure what the situation was. "Will they be coming with us?"

"I'm afraid not, sweet lady," Ross Senior said gently with a smile. "Just Nell and me. I'm already feeling a tightness gathering in my chest. I can't do with this climate much longer, whether I prefer it here or not."

"Then, what should I do?" Rosie pleaded, very unsure what she ought to do. Then it suddenly dawned on her that she had enough money to do both – at least six months in Southern France near to her father, and a month or two in England in the frozen wastes of The North Riding among her family – brother and niece. Perhaps she could even learn to…

"Penny for your thoughts, Rosie," her father asked, seeing that she was struggling with her decisions. Her explanation took him by surprise.

"What you're suggesting, then, is for you to split your living time between the South of France and the North of England?" he asked, his emotions working overtime. "It would be wonderful to be able to cement our relationship after so long each of us not knowing that the other one even existed. No pressure from me though. Whatever you decide will be fine, although we have only one week left here, and that means we – Nell and me – won't be returning here, ever again."

<hr>

"Father?" Rosie asked the day before he and Nell were due to retrace their steps to the Cote d'Azur.

"Yes, my dear, you can," he replied with an unexpected response that caught his daughter by surprise.

"I can … what?" she sought, not understanding what he was agreeing to.

"I have watched you puzzling with your dilemma – 'shall I/shan't I?' – since you arrived here, and I believe you have arrived at your decision," Ross Senior answered what seemed to be her insurmountable question.

"And my decision is?" she said with a challenging smile.

"I believe," her father said slowly, making her wait, "that you … will … spend the greater part of your year with … part of your family in … Europe."

"But both England and France *are* in Europe!" she insisted. "Is that the best you have?"

"Not finished what I was about to say," he interrupted, perpetuating the game with her.

"Well? Go on then!" she dared him.

Before saying another word, he handed her a large envelope with her name printed on its sealed flap.

"What's this for?" she coaxed, wanting him to state *his* choice before she opened the envelope.

"I think you need to open it, and then you'll know what I think," he challenged her.

She smiled in excitement as she began to open it slowly. Withdrawing its contents, she stopped, mouth agape and eyes wide in surprise.

"But … this is … a ticket for tomorrow to travel on the Train Bleu to Nice," she uttered, almost unable to believe what he had done. Not only had he chosen the right decision for her, but he had also purchased tickets for her to travel with them back to The French Riviera. "How did you … know?"

"I didn't, but to me it seemed the most logical and likely," he explained. "You had found the father that you wanted, and you came to find him … from Australia, where the climate is more like Southern France than Northern England. No brainer."

"Time to tell everyone else, then?" Rosie suggested tentatively.

"They have already worked it out," Ross laughed. "The cold North Riding is not the permanent year-round place to stay for a warm-blooded Aussie. Although I was born here, I lived for many years in the Antipodes. Nice is my preferred place to live, for as long as I have left."

"My case is packed and I'm ready to go, when you are," she said. "And, by the way, thank you very much for the tickets. Will they be for accommodation with you?"

"As close as we can make it," he replied. "For my daughter, Rosie."

"Well, Mrs Brown, here's the thing," Mary said once she and her husband had settled in Mrs Brown's very sparsely furnished front room. They had a cup of tea to hand, with Jimmy and sister Maisie sitting on the floor in front of them. "We have a food shop in the High Street called Mary's Pantry, and what we would like to do is to offer your daughter here, a job – if she is agreeable – in the new shop we are opening next door. While she is learning her new job, we will pay her weekly wage as enough food to feed you all for each week."

Mrs Brown gasped in utter surprise as tears began to gather.

"Once she has learned the job, we would pay her wage in money and food," Mary went on. "That, of course, is based upon Maisie's accepting what we are offering. We would also pay for her working clothes that would fit in with the other folks we employ. Maisie?"

Open-faced with mouth sagging in awe at what she had just heard, she nodded enthusiastically.

"What do I have to do?" Maisie sought, rather confused at the things normal folks do.

"We'll come for you sometime next week, if that's all right?" Mary acknowledged. "We are hoping the new shop will be ready within the next week or two, where you will be working with my niece, Mary-Jane."

"What the bluddy 'ell's goin' on 'ere?" an aggressively rough voice accosted them as they turned to leave, moving in on Geoffrey threateningly.

Maisie and Mrs Brown cowered, trying not to be seen.

"It's mi dad," Jimmy mouthed, trying not to be heard.

"This is my 'ouse!" the ruffian shouted, raising a short club of wood to threaten Mary and her husband. "So, gerout before I club you to death!"

As he raised the club ready to strike Geoffrey, an enormous hand gripped his wrist from behind, stopping the club before its downward fall towards Geoffrey's head.

A puzzled look set in the man's face before he started to turn round to see what was happening. Struggling to release himself, he turned fully, to be met by an enormous fist in his mouth, hurling him backwards against the open door.

Shaking his head slowly, he picked himself up with the club again raised, to be met by the same fist which burst his nose and mouth asunder, splattering blood and teeth in the doorway into which he collapsed unconscious.

"Ross?" Mary gasped. "How—?"

"I came to the shop to order a load of stuff and to ask if you would help us with a gathering this weekend," Ross explained. "I was told that you were here … fortunately."

Groans grew from the floor as the assailant began to stir and make to stand up. He was helped to his unsteady feet by Ross, whose enormous frame hoisted him upright. Standing at least six inches above the thug, he drew his face to his and, warning him of repercussions should he return, he threw him out bodily, knowing he would never return.

"I cannot thank you enough," Jimmy's mother said timidly. "This house isn't his and we never became man and wife. He just came in one day and took over. Perhaps we can now try to live some sort of a life."

Ross listened to their story quietly with more than a degree of compassion before he asked, "I can see that you have an injured leg, but is it a permanent injury?"

"Why do you ask?" she said, puzzled at his question.

"We are short staffed at our farm in the dairy, and I was wondering if you could … stand for a while," he explained. "It's quite a physically easy job, but you need to be able to stand."

"I can stand but too much movement of my knee can be painful," she replied with a grimace.

"We will be able to find you a sitting place, I am sure," Ross added. "Interested in good money, too?"

"I won't be able to travel from here because I have no transport and neither could I afford it if I had," she explained sadly.

"How would it be if we were to put you up in one of our spare cottages?" he persevered.

She looked at him, then at both daughter and son who were nodding eagerly.

"Well," she added, "if you can do that for us – we will pay our way with rent – then you have yourself a deal. We would love to get away from this … dump."

"We would come to some arrangement with Mary here as far as getting Maisie to work every day, so that wouldn't pose any problems," Ross went on, casting a glance at Mary who was nodding her assent.

"When do we start?" Mrs Brown asked. "You can see we have precious little in the furniture line."

"There is already a furnished cottage at Boulders Wood that has been empty for a little while," Ross offered with a winning smile. "We could start getting you in there … next week?"

"We?" Mrs Brown queried.

"Yes," Ross assured her. "*We* will move you, lock, stock and barrel."

CHAPTER 25

One very early morning in August, the ocean liner, The Blue Star, pulled away from the Liverpool's Prince's Landing Stage, ready to make its lengthy voyage into the unknown for most of its intrepid but innocent travellers. Viewed by many now as the Gateway to the West, its pilot tug guided its huge but sleek bulk out into the Irish Sea, it's triple funnels belching out thick streamers of black smoke from their coal-fired engines on the Tank Top deck below. Herring boats dotted the water, recognisable by their dark maroon sails billowing in the early summer breeze.

"Not too sure that this is really what I wanted to do so soon after London and Paris," Poppy muttered, more to herself than to Hal and Abigail, as they leaned over the rail on the Boat Deck where the lifeboats were stored and the entrance to the First-Class Grand Staircase could be found.

The Promenade Deck below them, extending almost the entire length of the ship's superstructure, was reserved exclusively for First-Class passengers, and contained First-Class cabins, the First-Class lounge, reading and writing rooms.

Here, too, the A la Carte restaurant and the Café Parisien provided luxury dining facilities for their First-Class passengers.

"How do you mean?" Hal asked carefully, not wishing to add to the pressures on his young friend's shoulders.

"Will this New York place offer me as much as London and Paris have done? Do we need to visit America *now*?" Poppy responded, very much unsure of herself. *Should* she have agreed to step into the dangerous unknown, bearing in mind that this was still a relatively new country even more unpredictable than her own. The journey across the Atlantic Ocean was also fraught with uncertainty.

"Don't take any notice of my quavering fears," Poppy urged her friends. "I know this is an opportunity not to be missed and I feel sure that once we are under way, we will thoroughly enjoy our two weeks together at sea. It's just that my feet are used to our relatively safe terra firma."

"We're here to give you as much support as you feel you need, dear Poppy," Abigail offered, putting her arm around her shoulders. "Once we get to New York, we will have the 'protection' we need from the company through whom you will be launching the book. No need to worry."

"In the meantime, we have almost a fortnight to enjoy our first-class voyage on this wonderfully comfortable floating hotel that has often been likened to the Ritz," Hal interjected, a huge grin of anticipation decorating his face.

Their rooms were incredibly luxuriously comfortable, designed with subdued elegance in the style of an English country manor or luxury hotel. These rooms were unusually large for a ship, and were equipped with the latest technologies for comfort, hygiene, and convenience. Recreational facilities like a saltwater swimming pool and a gymnasium were close at hand on their deck. This catered for Hal's predilection for exercise to allow him to eat the delicious delicacies on the menu.

Dressing table, wardrobe, horsehair sofa and marble topped washstand with basin were standard in their rooms. Most First-Class cabins, however, shared bathroom facilities, with communal lavatories having illuminated signage that were to be found along the passageways, divided by gender. Reservations had to be made with respective bedroom stewards to use one of the communal bathrooms.

Fortunately for Poppy, Hal had made it in his way to find out everything about … everything for their return journey. Consequently, they each had a cabin that boasted a private shower room. He had engaged two such cabins because it was the only way to 'bathe' using fresh water, whereas having a 'bath' meant the use of salt water.

"I'm going to have a lay down," Hal announced as the ship headed slowly for the open sea. "Lunch is in a couple of hours, and I need to be fresh and ready for what the menu suggests we might eat."

"See you later, then, dear Hal," Poppy said as he turned. "I at least need to see what's ahead and to take in this wonderful sea air."

"Me too," Abigail agreed, "We don't get this sort of fresh air on land."

*

"Hello," a deep voice joined Poppy once Abigail had left to take a rest with her husband.

Poppy's head swivelled quickly to see a startlingly green-eyed, very short-haired man sitting opposite her on one of the settees in the reading room.

"Hello?" she replied, a distinctly surprised tone in her voice.

"My name's Olleranshaw; Jeremiah Olleranshaw," he responded, causing a surprised catch in her voice. Strange that that name should crop up, here of all places.

"I knew an Olleranshaw ... once," she offered quietly. "He—"

"Was my cousin, Peter," the young man explained, equally quietly.

"Was?" Poppy queried, unsure about the tense.

"He was killed in a hunting accident several weeks ago," he acknowledged. "His wife—"

"Wife?" Poppy reacted in shock. "I didn't—"

"Know?" Jeremiah added. "Most people didn't, especially if they were lovely young ladies ... like you. We are still not too sure it was an accident."

"What was the context, if you don't mind my asking?" Poppy ventured, intrigued about a possible unlawful killing.

"Out shooting grouse, Peter's gun partner pointed his loaded twelve bore at his quarry, but the gun misfired," Jeremiah explained. "His partner examined the trigger mechanism, pressing it a couple of times, when the gun went off, hitting Pater in the chest. Killed him instantly."

"Sounds a bit—" Poppy grimaced in horror.

"Dodgy?" Jeremiah added with a slight inclination of the head. "Nothing can be proven other than it was an unfortunate accident. Yet..."

"Good gracious!" Poppy almost mouthed, wondering why this should have happened.

"The police are still investigating," he said with a shrug. "No evidence to the contrary as there was no-one else about, and they can't trace the grouse to elicit *its* testimony."

Poppy laughed quietly at the image in her mind of two police officers interrogating a large ... bird.

"Are you New York bound?" he went on when he had ordered a tot of whisky for him and a flute of some bubbly liquid for her.

"Indeed," she responded once she had the glass of bubbles to hand, a quizzical raising of the eyebrows expressing her surprise.

"Veuve Clicquot 1900," he replied. "One of the best Champagnes around."

This dragged her mind back to the last time she spent her late evening with an Olleranshaw. Enjoyable over drinks in a hotel's lounge but not so when events caught up with her much later.

"Book launch," she offered after the drink's bubbles had left her senses. "I am an—"

"Author?" he interrupted. "I know. I was around your bookshop in London, and in Garibaldi's in Paris."

"My word, that was indeed a … synchronicity of coincidences," Poppy uttered with a knowing smile. "And now … here. How did you manage all of that, Jeremiah Olleranshaw?"

He raised his forefinger to the side of his nose, and with a wicked chuckle curling his lips, he winked as he turned to head for the stairs.

"Olleranshaw, eh?" she mouthed as she, too, headed for her room. "Not sure about *that* family."

As she reached her cabin's door, Abigail slipped out of hers quietly.

"Poppy!" she almost whispered taking hold of her arm. "Quickly! Come in here!"

Once inside the McIntyre luxury cabin, gesturing for her to sit on the settee next to Hal, she waved a piece of paper in front of her eyes.

"Just had a wire from home to tell us that Peter Olleranshaw – you remember him? – has been shot and killed," Abigail urged.

"Yes, I do," Poppy replied quietly.

"You don't seem very shocked?" Abigail challenged. "Do you know something we don't?"

"I've just been talking to his cousin, Jeremiah, in the sitting lounge," Poppy responded. "Why? Anything wrong? He was telling me about how it had happened. Shooting party in the Dales, or something?"

"Not quite," Hal interjected. "Jeremiah is being sought for his … murder. And a reward of £300 has been posted."

Poppy stiffened stunned to hear that bit of – very important – news.

"How can this be?" she gasped as she told them where she had met him and why she had thought he was on this steamer.

"It could be that he is heading for cover in America, as it is such a large country," she continued. "He could effectively … *disappear*. Should we get in touch with the authorities. I mean—"

"What this Jeremiah didn't tell you is that he was – is – joint partner in Peter's company," Hal informed her. "With Peter out of the way, the company belongs to him, allowing him to sell to realise around one hundred thousand pounds. This could collapse our projects, particularly *this* jaunt in New York. He needs to be caught with the utmost speed."

"So much for a relaxing week or two on the high seas to the Americas!" Abigail sighed disappointedly.

Chapter 26

Ross Senior awoke at six o'clock almost every day. He didn't mind really because the sun almost always welcomed him as he stepped out onto their balcony which offered a glorious view across the Mediterranean's glinting surface. The only things he didn't enjoy were shaving – how he would love to have grown a beard! – and going to bed. Nell would never have allowed him to sprout a beard, and he felt he would like to get the maximum out of every day. Sleeping stopped him from doing that.

Nell had become used to sleeping in most days as a compensation for all those early starts in her days running a manic household and allowing her demanding husband to take his fill of her rapidly aging body.

Ross's usual routine was lather shave, cup of coffee outside for ten minutes or so, to be followed by preparing breakfast-in-bed for his wife. Creatures of habit, they liked to have choice of the usual items most French inhabitants would choose. This day he chose grapefruit juice with fruit compote to be followed by cereals and tartines de beurre, and a small drinking bowl of café au lait.

He had gotten used to the idea that plates were not used, as the slices of baguette which were smothered with butter were consumed over the coffee bowl, and frequently dipped into the liquid before eating. This had taken quite a lengthy period for them to become used to doing, as this was not a practice followed either in Australia or England.

Ross and Nell almost always breakfasted on their patio-like balcony which afforded them complete privacy without even a slight sideways glance from other inhabitants of this lovely town, and that Mediterranean view was to die for.

No sign of Nell yet gave him time to prepare everything she loved without the fear of interference from her. It had taken him a long time to inculcate this practice into her days until it was now *almost* always successful. This morning should be no different. He had to take it easy with most things he undertook because his lungs wouldn't allow him to overexert himself which might cause him a catastrophic break down if he did.

Slow and methodical did it for him.

Even at this time in the morning, the sun's rays were becoming almost overpowering for holidaying locals, with shade a must and skin protection necessary to enjoy outside living.

Ross inched his way into the bedroom, using his skinny backside as a lever for their gloriously oak door. Putting the laden tray on the small coffee table in the centre of this rather larger than necessary space, he cast a glance over at his wife as he crept across the room to release the bedroom's glass doors to its balcony. She was still and quiet which was usual for her as she was a very quiet sleeper.

The sunshine burst into the room enlivening this wonderful space after its inertly warm night.

Ross tip-toed to the bed, almost whispering her name so as not to shock her awake.

"Sweetheart?" he urged gently. "Our chef has prepared your favourite breakfast which awaits your lips. Sweetheart?"

He was unusually amazed at how long she was able to sleep, even with the early-to-bed regime they had been enjoying for the last year or two.

"Nell? Are you all right?" he said, reaching across to kiss her cheek. He gasped, recoiling in shock and dismay.

Her cheek was very cold, as was her entire body. He reeled backwards, falling and hitting his head on the coffee table, sending it and its contents skittling across the floor.

Dazed, after a few moments, he turned onto his hands and knees, his forehead resting on the floor, the realisation about the present situation flooding his numbing mind.

~

The front door clicked in the early afternoon as Rosie returned from a couple of days staying with Australian friends, she had met along the Promenade des Anglais. They were on their way to England to visit their ancestors' homeland when by chance they had met Rosie who was lunching with her father, Ross. The youngsters – two sisters and a brother – had hit it off immediately and had decided to spend some time together. Over the last few days, they had visited places in Nice and, generally, had had a good time.

"Father?" Rosie called as she walked through a somewhat darkened hallway towards the sitting room. Even the curtains were drawn, cutting out all light from the balcony. "Father? Are you there?"

"In the dining room," came his quiet and restrained answer.

She found him sitting in his favourite easy chair, a framed picture of his wife, Nell, resting in his lap.

"Why is everywhere in darkness? And where is Nell?" she asked, puzzled at all this subterfuge.

"She's gone," he responded after a moment or two's hesitation.

"Gone? "she asked still not understanding. "Where? Back to England?"

"I found her in bed the day before yesterday morning, cold and lifeless," he added as tears began to trickle slowly down his face. "As we are not allowed to keep her here any longer, she lies, undisturbed in the dark at the local mortuary, where she is not supposed to be, and I can no longer see her,"

"You mean, she's … gone … permanently?" Rosie gasped. "And we won't have the chance to see her … *again*?"

She rushed over to him, threw her arms about his neck and drew him to her.

"I am so, so sorry," she said quietly. "We must let her family know. *Then* what do we need to do?"

"I wired them yesterday," he observed. "Now there are certain rules with which we must abide according to French law. I have had to notify the mayoralty from where a physician was sent to examine her and determine the cause of death. We have to draw up the so called 'act of decease' which becomes an official document after which the mayor fixes the day and hour of the funeral."

"Is she to be buried … here?" Rosie puzzled, not sure whether she understood the rules and regulations of this sort of thing. "Wouldn't you want to take her back to England?"

"Two reasons why it will be here," he began to explain. "We live – lived – here because of my illness and because we liked it. Secondly, it would be impossible to take her back because it isn't a state funeral where a country pays for all the services to transport a body, and of course wouldn't you know it, it is legally not allowed, even if it were *financially* possible. She will be buried here, and I will follow in due course."

"You don't have to worry, Father," Rosie said, drawing him closer. "I will be here, and I *will* look after you."

*

"Thank you," Martha said to the telegram delivery man as she closed the door. Her husband had left for work around an hour before, and, as she knew he would be still in the barn, she slipped on her shawl and hurried out into a damp drizzly morning in the North Riding's unpredictable climate.

"Ross?" she shouted at the barn door. "Ross? You there?"

"Certainly am, my sweet," he returned jovially. "Is it snap time already?"

"As it happens … no," she replied with a laugh. "A telegram has just arrived for you."

"What does it say?" he added.

"It's addressed to you, personally," she replied.

"How many times…?" he sighed as he tore it open, but stopped talking as he read the missive, his face saddening as he did.

"Ross?" Martha said, a tone of misgiving in her voice, seeing the sadness in his face.

"It's from Father," he started quietly, a look of deep sadness overtaking his face. "'Mother died the day before yesterday STOP Funeral in one week STOP'."

"Oh Ross!" Martha said softly. "I'm so sorry."

"And we thought Father would be the first to go," he retuned quietly thoughtful. "I think I need to nip over to the cottage to warn Joseph."

He took her into his arms and kissed her passionately, noting mentally that his dear mother's departure should be a wakeup call to both brothers in their humdrum lives. His crunch along the pathway to their cottage seemed to take an age even with *his* giant stride.

"Not in, I'm afraid, Ross," Lilly Victoria said with a puzzled look. Her brother-in-law rarely called unless he had an urgent matter in hand that he needed his brother's say-so on how to proceed. What was *so* important now? "He won't be back, I should think, for another hour or so. Anything I can do?"

He gave her the news and the telegram, on the understanding that she would alert her husband as soon as he got back from whatever his business had involved. It would have been easier to plan their next move had Hal been to hand, but he was in—

"Poppy!" he blurted out as he rounded the path back to Boulders Wood's front door, realising that there was no way he could contact his niece to deliver the bad news.

Hearing his distinctively huge stride on the gravel, Martha had already mashed a pot of tea and dug out one of his favourite buns from the pantry.

"Poppy!" he called again as he gained the front room.

"Is either still on the boat, or is in New York, book launching," his wife added. "No way of contacting her."

"If we tried to message her there would be no way she could reach Nice in time for the funeral anyway," Ross answered. "We need to decide how we will get there as well. I need to talk to Joseph."

CHAPTER 27

Poppy was overwhelmed and awe-stricken when they arrived at their hotel. Still light for mid-evening but more than a little chilly as they prepared to enter the foyer of their luxurious Hotel Astor in Manhattan on Time Square and Broadway between 44th and 45th Street. She had never seen anything quite like this before. The last few days on the Blue Star had disappeared in a whirl of exciting social events that would have made any young British socialite steam with envy. Now she was about to become immersed in her true nirvana, heaven upon Earth. How she wished her dear friend, Florence, was here to share it with her.

"How wonderful is this magnificent building," Poppy eulogised about what was before her incredulous eyes. "You can't half pick 'em, my dear Hal. How did you know about this one?"

"Personal experience, I believe," Abigail suggested, always sure that he had either been there or knew someone else that had.

"It's the only one that's close enough to Jake Russell's Ortheus Bookstore on 4th Avenue," Hal explained. "4th Avenue

is known locally as **_Book Row_** because there are so many of
them there.”

“Then why that one?” Poppy asked.

“It’s the best for our purpose,” he retorted. “Almost all
the other ones are antiquarian or second-hand shops, and
Faithfully Yours falls into neither category … yet.”

“Our hotel,” he went on, “is French style inspired and was
built in 1905, so not so long ago.”

“I find it all fascinating,” Poppy rejoiced as they approached
the desk.

“Bounded by Broadway, Shubert Alley and 44th and
45th Streets, it was built in what they call the ‘Beaux-Arts
Architectural Style’,” Hal continued. “To put it simply, it has
classical Greek and Roman columns, pediments and balus-
trades to create a grand and imposing façade.”

“Pediments?” Abigail sighed. This was too much even for her.

“Triangular gable centre points above entrances,” he
explained. “Did you notice that the triangular point was
uppermost with columns underneath?”

“This is even better than the hotels in London and Paris!”
Poppy gasped, eyes wide in wonderment.

“We have one day to finalise and prepare, and then the
day after tomorrow … it’s the signing and launch, followed
the day after that by embarkation and the return journey,”
Hal announced. “So, we have dinner tonight in the Rooftop
Garden restaurant, followed by entertainment and the odd
glass of wine. There is also something I want us to see.”

“And what is that Husband dear?” Abigail queried, a little
surprised that he had kept something to himself that she knew
nothing about.

“You’ll see when we sit down for dinner,” he confided,
looking over both shoulders as he winked. “And, Poppy, when

the bell boy brings your luggage to your room it is customary to tip him."

"Bell boy? Tip him?" she asked, not really having come across those terms before. "Will he have a bell around his neck, and then should I tip him down the stairs?"

"That is a question I am able to answer, Madam," a cultured American voice cut in. "My name is Lewis; Jerry Lewis, and I look after our customers, here behind the reception counter."

"Good day, Mr Lewis," Poppy responded with a smile. "Bell boy? Tip?"

"The term came into common use in 1897 when hotels decided to employ general uniformed dogsbody employees in the foyer to do general stuff like carrying luggage and showing customers to rooms," he started to explain. "Because they might be anywhere in the hotel, we would summon them by ringing a bell which they had to 'hop to' – hence 'bell hopper' or now 'bell hop'. As they became younger, the 'boy or adolescent male' became known as 'bell boy'."

"Fascinating!" Poppy said, clapping her hands quickly and quietly. "Tip?"

"A small amount of cash in hand for him, forming part of his wage," the receptionist explained finally. "Probably a couple of cents or so. Whatever you as the valued customer might decide."

"Thank you," Poppy said. "Most interesting."

"Can I take it, Miss Spence, that you are the latest very popular author to cross our threshold?" he went on.

"Indeed, you can," Abigail butted in, "And believe me when I say she will be very much appreciated in New York. She sold thousands in London and Paris, and she is likely to do the same here. Are you a reader, may I ask?"

"Not so much me, as my wife," he countered. "She loves romance and such like."

"Then she will be delighted with ***Faithfully Yours*** by Poppy Spence," Abigail emphasised. "Book launch for America here at Ortheus Bookshop on 4th Avenue, or 'Book Row' as it's known locally. Starts day after tomorrow at ten am. I suggest you or your wife might like to get there early because if you don't, the queue will be lengthy and slow-moving."

The rooms were astonishingly luxurious and comfortable, giving Poppy enough time to relax and just … sit, with a flute of fizzy something she never did at home.

It was fortunately warm and dry outside, allowing them to dine in the open air on the flat, green copper roof.

Walking into the space to dine, Poppy and Abigail stopped in their tracks suddenly, both turning to share puzzled looks with Hal. In front of them, in a side part of the restaurant, a very lengthy table had been set out, around which sat thirty older men each dressed in evening suit, white shirt and black bow tie. At the very far end of the table sat a group of young women, also dressed in evening attire, as if waiting for … something.

Poppy whispered to Hal with a shrug, "Are all these … people … together?"

"Only in a certain way," Hal replied with a grin. "You see, this is a Debutante Presentation Dinner."

"Have they all won prizes that are about to be presented to them?" she went on, unable to work out what was about to happen.

"Actually, no," he explained. "These are very wealthy businessmen waiting to introduce their eligible daughters to society gentlemen with a view to future marriage."

"I don't believe it!" Poppy gasped quietly so as not to be either over-heard or thought to be in the market for a young husband. "You can't be serious!"

"It's how it's done worldwide, actually, Poppy," Abigail agreed. "*We* live in a different world."

"Shall we move to our table where all we want to do is eat?" Hall suggested. "Just wanted to show you how the other – upper – half lives."

~⸙~

"We need to agree, then, that you boys must go to Nell's funeral and to support Ross Senior, while we will remain here to look after the farms and the nippers," Lilly Victoria insisted, to vigorous nods from Martha.

"But—!!" Joseph complained.

"No buts," Martha joined in. "There is no need for us to be there hundreds of miles away, and who would look after the children if we weren't here?"

"We can't take them with us," Lilly Victoria insisted. "All that travelling—"

"And all that expense," Martha butted in. "It's a nonsense. Besides, I'm expecting, and it wouldn't do—"

Ross turned sharply, a smile growing. "Can only agree then," he said drawing his wife towards him in a gentle hug. "We are expecting another nipper?"

"Actually, no," she corrected him. "*I* am expecting. Travelling now would not be a good idea."

Forming in a hugging group around Martha, they all heaped their praise on her bravery, bringing a suffusion of pink to her cheeks, almost in embarrassment.

"Settled, then," Ross reacted firmly. "I will book our tickets and—"

"No need," Lilly Victoria said quite firmly, as Joseph threw a surprised look towards his brother. "I have made your booking. Train to London, ferry across the English Channel, Blue Train – overnight – to Nice. Two days starting later this evening."

"You two need to pack, then," Martha smiled, satisfied with their reaction to what she and her sister had planned all along. "Not much time left, or your mother will be seen off before you have time to breathe."

Chapter 28

"Not the sort of bookshop I might have expected in this brave new world," Poppy observed as she settled behind the customary table, a pile of books to either side of her. "It looks and smells like I would expect a bookshop in Charles Dickens' time to have looked."

"It might be a little … unorthodox for its age, but I think it's exactly how it *should* look," Abigail said with a nod.

"The queue I was expecting outside is somewhat … smaller than I thought it might be, perhaps," Poppy continued, a mixed look of controlled excitement and mild disappointment licking around her eyes.

"No need to concern yourself about that," a deeply resonant voice poured over her shoulder. She looked around sharply to notice a tall thin man with a curly bush of uncombed hair decorating the top of his head. His magnificently tailored black beard covering the lower half of his face just allowed a bright red dicky bow to peek through. From his dark blue waistcoat buttonhole there hung a gold Albert that no doubt was attached to an ornate golden pocket watch that hid in his waistcoat … pocket. "New Yorkers never seem to do the things you might expect. Jacob Russell at your service – but you can call me Jake."

"I'm sorry Mr Russell – Jake – I didn't see you there," Poppy apologised. "Not many takers today?"

"No need to concern yourself, Miss Poppy Spence," he replied enthusiastically. "I have read your book, and trust me, they will have heard about it too. Arriving in about an hour in their droves, they are literature guzzlers, and my only concern is that we may not have enough books to satisfy our eager customers."

"Trust me, my friend," Hal assured him. "We have stocks already waiting to be delivered. We will have more than enough."

"Here goes!" Jake Russell called out, making his way to unlock the door and let in the mini hordes of 'guzzling' literature lovers.

～⌒～

The steady trickle of book-hungry customers lasted until half an hour before midday when Hal took it upon himself to have a look outside to see how much more of the small queue remained. He had thought that they might be finished in time for lunch in one of the cafes close by.

"My God!" he gasped, not able to take in what lay before his unbelieving eyes. Stretching down one side of 4th Avenue, north to Union Square and south to Astor Place, the queue measured probably five hundred yards or so, all readers in good humour and spirits.

Both Hal and Abigail recognised that this was Poppy's show and so secreted themselves behind a large set of bookshelves by the door so they would be able to watch, unseen, how things were going.

Poppy had been signing and talking to her customers for an hour or so, with a cashier taking care of the sales, when a commotion burst out. A smallish fellow barged his way to the front of the queue, brandishing a pistol, the sort of which any cowboy would have been happy to carry.

"Stay where you are!" he shouted in broad Manhattan, "and hand over the money! Now!"

Everyone in the queue froze in fear because most of them had either witnessed or been told about this sort of occurrence which seemed to happen all too frequently.

As soon as the gun came out and the words were yelled, the man collapsed to the floor, unconscious, blood oozing from a gash just over his left ear. The whole crowd in the shop stood, looks of amazement and shock flicking from face to face, until they saw that Abigail still had her walking stick to hand which had snapped as its thick wooden stock had met the prospective robber's skull.

Immediately, a deafening cheer of approval spread through the crowd, with some laughing and others applauding this brave British broad.

The police were called, and the miscreant carted away in handcuffs, still unconscious.

During all this time, unabashed, Poppy had continued book signing and engaging her public, it had all happened so fast. She was able to meet her self-set target with no problem. Jake Russell was almost right when he realised, at the end of all the excitement there remained only one copy of **Faithfully Yours**, and that belonged to him, containing as he proudly noticed a splash of blood across the front cover. That one was never going to leave *his* hands!

"Abigail?" Hal said to her quietly when they were on their way to the hotel, "How on earth did you manage to do *that?*

Talk about quick!"

"I saw him come in, shouldering his way through our crowds that had been queuing for ages," she explained. "That was just rude! Then I noticed the gun, and the rest was almost an automatic reaction."

"Certainly was!" Poppy laughed. "Remember when those thugs broke into my cottage?"

"Too right," Abigail giggled.

"Thugs?" Hal puzzled. "Broke into—?"

"Tell you later, lovely man," Abigail offered. "Time to eat. I'm starving."

Never having travelled by train – or even travelled anywhere – before, Joseph and Ross found following a tight timetable extremely difficult. They had always been governed by the ultimate timetable – Nature herself. They didn't find man-made rules important, particularly Ross with his usual way of working and living. Normally the brothers spent little of their time in idle conversation because time was money to them. Consequently, their journey to London was spent largely in either silent contemplation or … asleep.

"Not sure whether this journey will serve any useful purpose," Joseph muttered as the French countryside whistled past them.

"It will for me, and should for you," Ross started more forcibly. "She was our mother who brought us up equally through difficult times for *her*, protecting us from the monster that was your, and purported to be my father. *I* also need to support *my* true father in these troubling times. Are you not enjoying the journey? Foreign country and all that?"

"The only pleasure I am getting from this Blue Train thing

is the amount of sleep it affords me," Joseph replied off-hand-edly. "Boredom is beginning to set in, and I am continuing to miss my family. You?"

"Of course, I am, but Ross is my family too," his brother returned quietly. "And so is the mother we are about to bury. She was a living part of *our* family a few days ago. How life can change the path we take, eh?"

"I'm not too sure about this French food either," Joseph grumbled.

"Or this foreign wine!" Ross added. "Give me a good old pint of ale anytime."

"They don't seem to have any sheep in the fields that we have travelled through," Joseph announced with surprise.

"No cows much in this south part we are in now, as well," Ross agreed. "How can they call this farming country?"

"Probably because the country on the whole seems to be much bigger than ours, farming has become influenced by how much space they have to grow crops and the like," Joseph surmised. "I'm sure *I* wouldn't like to farm here."

"We're slowing down … and I can smell the sea!" his brother said with an element of surprise in his voice. "Look!"

They scrambled to catch sight of and gasp at the vastness of the sea along whose coast the train had now begun to travel. The sun was warm through the window they had opened, and a gentle breeze caught them as they pulled into and slowly through a smallish town with a strangely spelled name.

"That's not how we spell 'cans' at home!" Joseph pointed out. "Imagine what our shop keepers would say if we used 'cannes' to ask for tins of vegetables, eh?"

"I think Father told me that that particular station – Cannes – was the stop before theirs – Nice," Ross tried to explain with a grin. "I wonder if it is a *nice* place. Nice place? Get it?"

"Yes, I did, and that was about as funny as cans and tins," Joseph scoffed. "Look! Over by that notice! Isn't that your father?"

"It is," his brother agreed, rather sad to see such a lonely-looking figure. "We need to get ready to disembark."

"Hark at you!" Joseph laughed. "Disembark all of a sudden. Sounds like a tree shedding its skin rather quickly."

"Thank you for coming, Chaps," Ross Senior said as soon as they had shaken hands. "Interesting journey into an extremely foreign land?"

"Yes, indeed," Ross agreed.

"No, not at all," his brother said at the same time.

"Funeral tomorrow, I'm afraid," Ross's father informed them. "Then you'll be on your way back, I suppose."

"Unfortunately," Joseph said. "We'll have a lot of work to catch up with when we get back. You know how it is."

"Can we see … Mother?" Ross asked as they entered the taxi to take them to his father's home. "Is she at home?"

"'Fraid not," Ross Senior returned quietly. "It's not allowed. Too hot, I'm afraid. It would cause the body to decompose rapidly. She's in the mortuary. It's a matter of having enough ice to keep things cool."

"Ice?" Joseph asked sharply. "What's ice got to do with it?"

"Too much would be used, and that has a cost implication," Ross Senior explained.

"You can afford it, can't you?" Joseph replied sharply with a frown.

"That's not the point," Ross's father said. "It's the law, and, as visitors to this country, we have to abide by rules and regulations. We're here."

The taxi slowed to a halt and as they disembarked, to be met by Ross's sister, Rosie, who hugged her brother as they both wept at their loss.

Chapter 29

"You both certainly have made a name for yourselves," Hal told his two ladies once they were back on board the Blue Star the day after the book launch in Ortheus Books on 4th Avenue. He explained that the social buzz thereabouts concerned the English lady that had incapacitated a prospective armed robber in a bookshop on 'Book Row' by creasing his skull with a walking cane. The most astonishing thing also was that the other *young* English lady author carried on book signing and dealing with her readers not six feet from this activity.

"The newspapers have been full of it, and Jake Russell not only has dealt with it, but has made much of the incident, drawing hundreds of his fellow New Yorkers to his shop and, more importantly for you, my dear Poppy, to your book," he continued.

"Sales, then, Hal?" Abigail asked with a face-splitting grin.

"To date, just before we boarded, Jake sent me a note to say that, during the launch, not only had he taken the money for one thousand and nine hundred copies, but he also keeps getting more orders throughout the day," Hal assured them, much to Poppy's unbounded delight. "The strong likelihood is that you will be invited back before long to replicate your success. I took a few little Brownie snaps which I will develop and send on to him."

"Hal!" Abigail said with a semi-serious and deprecating tone.

"It all happened so quickly, that it was close to being an automatic reaction," he said, defending himself. "It was almost as if my little camera took over and I had no choice but to do as I was bidden."

"What happened to the miscreant?" Poppy asked, still mesmerised by everything that had happened to her in the last few days – as if everything else was a minor occurrence.

"Hospitalised unconscious first," Hal answered. "Then he awoke in a dingy police cell wondering why he was there and why he had such a pounding headache."

They all laughed at the image that had been created, not sure why this had happened to three ordinary English people. Poppy was so pleased with herself she couldn't stop smiling. She was convinced, even, that the smile would still be there when she was asleep.

"You do realise, of course, my dear Abigail and Hal, that had it not been for you, none of this would have happened," Poppy acknowledged over afternoon tea in the First-Class lounge. "I wonder what everyone at home might be doing, and how Nanny Nell and Grandpa Ross are enjoying their relaxing time in their beautiful home on the French Riviera in Nice?"

"Probably what we are doing here – having a lovely cup of tea and a spot of your nanny's delicious Victoria sponge cake," Hal answered, the remembered taste of all the cakes she baked shouldering its way back into his mind. What he would give for even a small piece of that cake now! "Don't forget, Poppy, that there would have been nothing for us to do had you not proved to be a superb writer and have the wherewithal to pay for all this."

"We've had a wonderful time since you crossed our path," Abigail butted in. "For one thing, Hal and I would never have met, we wouldn't have had our lovely daughter, and we would not have visited so many exciting places together."

"I can't wait to tell Nanny Nell about it all," Poppy gushed. "She'll be so pleased to understand how happy all this has made me."

She settled back into her easy chair and closed her eyes to glory in her happiness. Three book launches in two capital cities and one hugely important metropolis that have allowed her to gather success after success. It doesn't get much better than that.

$\sim$

"Ger 'im!" a roughly spoked voice growled as three ruffians broke into the sitting room of one of the elegant houses in Richmond. They obviously knew their target was in because of the disability he had suffered some time before.

The room was in darkness, so they weren't sure. They had dealt with him before, and as he was a slippery character to put it mildly, they knew they had to take care. One of them opened a curtain slowly, and as he did three loud spits of fire issued from a Browning pistol, causing two bodies to thud to the floor with bullets to the head, allowing the third to escape covered in blood. No further sound was heard other than the clattering of the open front door in the gathering breeze.

$\sim$

"Errand successful, Toby?" Jenny asked him as they rounded the corner to their house. She always looked forward to getting back home because she had never had one before, particularly not one as gloriously elegant as this one. She was convinced that Jonas was at last hers and that they loved each other dearly. Shame about his missing leg, but life plods along, and it didn't seem to cause him any discomfort lately.

"Yes, Mother," her son replied, pleased that his new stepfather was leaning on him more and more, trusting his new-found son would carry out all his requests honestly. It seemed strange that Jonas's attitude towards honest endeavour had about-faced, allowing him to become an upstanding member of his new-found society – something they thought would never happen.

Jenny stopped in her tracks suddenly, concerned that the front door was openly swaying in the gathering breeze.

"Why is the door open?" she whispered in fear, feeling that something may be amiss.

"Pops probably wants a bit of air," Toby returned. "You know how oppressive it can get when he has the fire blazing at full heat."

"Blood on the front door handle?" she said. "Now do you think everything is all right? Careful!"

Ushering his mother to stay behind him, Toby opened the door slowly, hoping any creak would not give him away. He followed the splashes of blood on the floor towards the sitting room where he could see two bodies sprawled either side of the door, eyes open and face covered in blood.

As she hesitated a moment on the threshold before entering, she screamed, a look of abject horror gripping her face. Sitting on the settee, Jonas's eyes staring in stark terror, mouth trying to speak and hand desperately begging for help, they could see the handle of a large knife sticking from the right-hand side of his chest, its blade buried up to its haft causing his clothes around it to have become crimson.

"Jonas! No!" she screamed as she reached for him.

His hand fell to his lap and his eyes closed as his chin fell forward and he stopped breathing.

"No!" she screamed again as she fell forward and passed out.

~

"At last, another pain in the arse gets his just deserts," the police constable sneered as Jonas's body was taken away for study and recording before the post mortem. "I have to say though, I didn't have him down as a gun man. The Browning is not a cheap piece, and not readily available to any Tom, Dick or Harry."

"Can you tell me what led up to this state of affairs, Mrs Jamieson?" Inspector Shaw asked in the study, away from the crime scene.

"We – my son and I – had gone out, me to the local shops and him to run an errand for his father," Jenny explained. "When we came back, we were met by what you saw next door. He'd had threats before which he had always sorted out. But now…"

"Did you recognise any of the attackers?" the policeman suggested. "Had you seen any of them before?"

"No, and I didn't know he possessed a gun, either," she insisted.

"I did," Toby butted in.

"Which?" the policeman asked very quickly, a glimmer of hope in his eyes.

"Both," the lad said. "I recognised one of the attackers and

I knew about the gun. The man you perhaps need to interview is called Pieter van de Behr, and he is the landlord at the Shady Lady Inn. They had had a number of … disagreements in recent history. The last one ended with de Behr threatening to kill Mr Jamieson. There was no love lost between them, I have to say. He might just be the one behind all of this.”

“Interesting,” Inspector Shaw muttered as he wrote down all the lad had offered. “Anything else?”

“You might perhaps like to have a look at George Garside,” Toby offered casually. “They had history. He was the man that shattered my dad’s leg and obliged him to have it cut off. I *know* Garside hated Mr Jamieson, and he too threatened to do him harm.”

He watched the policeman jotting down what he had been telling him, a secret smile lurking, giving him satisfaction that Jonas’s nemesis would have a lot of trouble from the police at least to cause disruption to his ordered life, if not to arrest him for the planned execution.

“I think you’ll find him—” the lad continued.

“I *know* where to find him, young man!” the policeman butted in sharply. “I may need to talk to you again, too, so don’t leave the area.”

Chapter 30

"Ow do, George. How's things?" Ross greeted friend and partner.

"All rayt, I suppose," George responded. "Sorry to hear about your mam, and your dad's illness. I know what you all must be feeling, and you have my deepest sympathy and condolences. I don't seem to have had much time to see any of you lately – early start and usually very late finish. That's t'top and bottom o' mi life these days. Poppy?"

"Don't know, really," Ross returned, "She's on her way back from America and should be with us in a few days."

"America?" George gasped in wonder. "That's a long way to go for a holiday, isn't it?"

"Not a holiday, my friend," Ross replied with a smile. "Book launching more like. Apparently in the depths of New York, wherever that is. Gone with her friends Hal, her cousin, and his wife, Abigail. She's allus wanted to write books, and this one seems to be doing well. Bit on a trailblazer, I believe."

"Summat I wanted to leave with you for us to discuss reasonably soon," George offered.

"Oh aye?" his friend said more than a little intrigued. "Any hints?"

"Just one," George advised. "I want to get rid o t'cows and t'dairy, so I can move into and concentrate on … sheep."

"Sheep?" Ross noted with something of a surprised look about him. "What do you intend to do that for? Any *real* reasons other than it's an integral part of *our* partnership that was set up wi' your dad all those years ago?"

"That's just it," he reacted. "It wor set up all those years ago by somebody else who wornt me, and it seems, on our part, to have dropped on my shoulders alone to manage – wi'out help I might add. Don't forget, Ross, that I alone have been responsible for widening our client base which has meant damned hard work and extremely long hours. Travelling about this extended area day in day out has tekken its toll on my personal life. I needn't remind you of the personal heartache I have had to endure while I've been gallivantin' about trying to make money for *our two* farms."

"What's next then?" Ross asked, understanding where he was coming from. "Desk job in an office? Sweeping roads?"

The sarcastic way Ross was trying to brush away George's concerns, didn't sit well with him.

"I want to rid *my* farm of cows and dairies and the like," he snapped. "Do you want 'em or shall I put 'em on to t'market?"

"I'll have to talk to Joseph about that one," Ross said, realising that his 'say-it-as-you-see-it' Yorkshireness wasn't working with another Yorkshireman. "If we do, what do you intend to do after that? Set up in competition?"

"Actually, no," George replied as he turned to leave. "I intend to bring in a reasonable flock of sheep. Well, two flocks actually; one of Swaledales and another of Herdwicks. Both on 'em are well used to steep hills and inclement weather, so they should settle and grow."

"Bloody 'ell!" Ross whistled, not having expected that. "Sheep, eh?"

"Aye," George reiterated. "It's what I've allus thought we ought to be doing. Swaledales particularly are well suited to exposed areas and upland farms – which we are – in our North Riding."

"I've heard on Swaledales," Ross puzzled. "But Herdwick?"

"T'name comes from old Norse 'herdvyck' which means 'sheep pasture'," George explained. "T'majority on 'em are in Cumberland and Westmoreland, but it's onny a cock stride to ower 'ere."

"'Ark at you! Owd Norse, eh?" Ross said quietly. "Interesting. Well, good luck wi' that un."

"Herdwick above all others, have the ability to look after themselves in all types of weather, including deep snow," George finished. "All rayt? I'm off now. Si thi."

With that George turned on his heels and walked off to his own farm to spend a bit of time with his remaining family … and Annabel.

~

"Anybody home?" George called as he bustled through into the front room. "Anybody off to mek me a cup of tea and a slice of bread and jam? Hello?"

Almost immediately a beautiful young lady entered from the kitchen bearing a tray laden with a large plate of sandwiches, a steaming teapot, two mugs, all surrounded by homemade buns, tarts and cake. She placed them on the table and indicated to him that the fire needed stoking up.

"Bloomin 'ummer, Annabel, I didn't expect such a feast!"

he said as he poked the fire's almost dead embers and piled on more wood to enliven the flames.

"Shall I take 'em back and distribute them among the staff then?" she replied with a cheeky grin. He walked over to her purposefully and, pulling her towards him, he kissed her fully on the lips, allowing her to sink towards him in acceptance. Once they had come up for air, she said with a delighted gasp, "I didn't expect that!"

"I'm sorry," he apologised. "I didn't mean—"

"Oh yes you did, and I'm glad of it," she returned. "I've been waiting for that for some time. I know our relationship in the early days, before you took up with my sister, didn't get off to a wonderful start, and I have no idea why I moved away from you. I realised shortly after that event that I had made a serious mistake. By the time we could have got together again, you had married Alice."

"Will you marry me, dear Annabel" he returned baldly. "I haven't been able to ask you before because of our history and because I didn't know whether you might be interested and—"

"Can we think about it for now, dear George?" she replied, kissing him on the cheek, but feeling a slight stiffening resistance from him.

"Sorry, I shouldn't have said," he returned, embarrassed he had asked and been rejected … again. He stood up slowly and turned to leave.

"George?" she urged, regretting almost immediately what she had said. "I didn't mean…!"

He didn't stop to listen, but headed for the front door, back to work.

～

"Sheep, did you say?" Joseph asked his brother, a degree of disbelief etching his face. "How the hell did he arrive at that conclusion? He must be—"

"He seems to have worked it all out, and it sounds very feasible," Ross answered him. "I've spoken to a number of folks who are experts in this field – Harry Prentice being one on 'em. You know him. He's from close on the border with Westmoreland and he's been in t'sheep business nigh on all his working life."

"Oh aye?" Joseph said, paying little attention while eating.

"Now then, do we want his cows, and to tek ower t'dairy?" Ross asked. "We've got capacity for t'cows and space for a dairy ower here."

"Whatever you think, Brother," was Joseph's answer, finally joining in the conversation. "I'll leave it to you. Now I must be away. I've t'boss man to see at yon bank in town."

With that he was up and away.

"I wonder," he muttered to himself. "Would it be possible to have a sheep farm as a part of Boulders Wood?"

***

"What a time we've had in America!" Poppy eulogised as she entered Boulders Wood's big house. Abigail and Hal had dropped her off and had set off to pick up their daughter from Abigail's mother's place. "This is a reception committee and a half."

She looked around the sitting room to see Ross and Martha, Joseph and Lilly Victoria, and Mary sitting quietly.

"Somebody died?" she joked looking at their dour and sombre faces, which didn't change at all.

Ross explained the situation to her slowly, taking care not to over emphasise anything unless she asked for details. They all sat in silence waiting for some sort of an emotional reaction from her, but, apart from the occasional tear, she remained still and thoughtful … and in control.

"They had to hold the funeral while Ross and I were there," Joseph explained, "because it's France when all said and done, and they have rules that have to be observed and obeyed."

"When?" Poppy asked calmly.

"Fortnight or so ago?" he said looking at Ross for corroboration. "We didn't want to let you know because it would have spoiled your time in America, and there was no way you could have done anything about the funeral."

"We wouldn't have known where to send any communication anyway," Ross added. "You didn't leave us any addresses for telegrams and such like."

Again, Poppy fell into silence, not really wishing to have such conversations. Her Nanny Nell was dead. How could discussing that make any difference now? It didn't matter about the intricacies. She was no longer here, and nothing could be done to change that.

It was then that probably the most momentous decision she had ever made jumped into her head. She would up sticks and move closer to Grandpa Ross in Southern France, as there was no longer anything here in the North Riding to keep her. Hal and Abigail had coaxed the world to drop into her lap, and, as they had become inveterate nomads, they would be able to call to see her on the Cote d'Azur.

In the meantime, she would be able to spend time with her Nanny Nell, and of course her Grandpa Ross without whose help and support she wouldn't have been able to achieve what she had.

"I have decided that I need to revisit Grandpa Ross in Nice and to visit where Nanny Nell is at rest," Poppy announced as the gathering was breaking up.

"Nice?" Ross asked, almost disbelieving what he had just heard. "But you've only just returned from the other side of the world. Don't you think you ought to stay here for a while? I mean…"

"Now's the right time, I am sure," she replied, a resolute gleam in her eyes.

"But you can't be thinking you'll travel all that distance on your own," Lilly Victoria warned. "It's not safe for a woman on her own, surely?"

"Abigail and Hal and little Grace have assured me that, if at any time I should feel the need to travel, they will accompany me. She is almost like a mind reader is Abigail. I shall stay here another two weeks and then I will take the Train Bleu as before," Poppy stated emphatically.

That announcement silenced the gathering, with most believing it was no more than a shocked reaction. Martha had different views. *She* had always admired Poppy's single-mindedness and the fact that she never gave up on her close-held ambitions. She *knew* that this might be the last time they would see her.

Chapter 31

The day was bright and dry with the promise of a reasonable temperature rise over the next week or so. Poppy had cleared away everything she didn't need on her journey to the French Riviera but had packed enough of the necessary things to make life bearable. Like change of clothing and cleansing toiletries and such like. The most important things, of course, were her writing materials that she couldn't do without. She knew she would be able to acquire a new Remington typewriter quite easily in France, so hers had to be locked away.

Looking around her cottage, perhaps for the last time, brought back memories she had shared with her dear friend, Florence; their time as youngsters when they spent Christmas as eight-year-olds; when they spent Poppy's twelfth birthday in and around Yorkshire's East Coast holiday hotspots; their Grand Tour in Europe where they covered two major capital cities and several chateaux along the Loire Valley. *She* would have loved New York with its garish hustle and bustle, and the folks who were in your face from morning to night. What a sadness that *she* wasn't able to achieve *her* goals.

She was drawn slowly out of her reverie by a gentle tapping at the front door. The taxi, perhaps ready to take her to Abigail and Hal's house just outside Richmond?

"George!" she said in quiet surprise that he had decided to come around. "How good to see you after what seems like such a long and overdue time."

"I hear you are off to sunny Southern France?" he queried once they had embraced. "Holiday? Or writing?"

"Both, really, and I need to spend time with Grandpa Ross and his daughter, Rosie," she explained. "It's important, too, to see where my Nanny Nell has been laid to rest."

"You certainly get around," he returned with a nod and a smile. "Are you happy? You've always had particular ambitions that none of us could ever have achieved – except for … Florence."

He stopped, a tear or two threatening to gather. Poppy put her arms around him and drew him to her. At one time this embrace would have led to much more, but this was about one friend comforting another.

"You and Annabel?" Poppy asked quietly, hoping he was about to discover that elusive happiness he had been chasing almost all his adult life. He didn't answer.

"Do you remember when you saved me from Jonas when we were in our teens?" she said, a wave of nostalgia beginning to creep upon them.

"That was the first time I fully realised I wasn't keen on him as a human being," he observed with a distasteful grimace.

"Is that what you called a fist in the face?" she laughed.

"Well, he asked for it – attacking my girls like that!" he responded.

"Did I hear that he had reached a grizzly end?" she asked.

"Aye. At least it was a knife in the chest, and not in the back like mine," he scoffed, the hate still lingering in his eyes.

"And that time we were coming home from school, and you fought off that monster that had grabbed me?" she shuddered. "God knows what he would have done to me if you hadn't been there to save me."

"Annabel and I are to be married, Poppy," he said almost in a whisper. "I had always felt that you and I were meant to be together, but other ... stuff ... intruded. Still, I will always carry you in my heart as a friend whom I will always look out for."

"George," she said quietly as she kissed him gently on the lips, catching him by surprise. He looked into her eyes one more time before turning on his heels and heading for the door, leaving her with tears gathering pace down her cheeks. He strode off into the distance not wanting her to see *his* tears and the painful emotions overloading *his* face.

"Was that George I saw leaving?" Abigail's excited voice wrapped itself around her. "Taxi awaits, milady."

One last look at the inside of her cottage where she had had so many conflictingly emotional episodes, and she hurried to the taxi, leaving Hal to lock up.

"Grace! How lovely to see you again," Poppy said as she hugged the little girl she now held as her niece. "Are you ready for another adventure?"

Feelings now free of all constraints, she settled back into the taxi's comfortable seats, her luggage loaded, yet her mind *unloaded,* as thoughts of Louisa May Alcott's description of the Promenade des Anglais in Nice in **Little Women** flooded her mind.

Thoughts of *the wide walk, bordered with palms, flowers and tropical shrubs* on one side and the Mediterranean Ocean on the other, filled her with excitement.

Her final description of the many nations and languages

and costumes proving to be a spectacle on a sunny day's joy, gripped Poppy's imagination.

That's where she wanted to be!

"Home, Hal, and don't spare the horses!" she urged finally with a grin, as Boulders Wood and all it stood for, disappeared quickly behind her.

Frank English
Author

Born in 1946 in the West Riding of Yorkshire's coal fields around Wakefield, he attended grammar school, where he enjoyed sport rather more than academic work. After three years at teacher training college in Leeds, he became a teacher in 1967. He spent a lot of time during his teaching career entertaining children of all ages, a large part of which was through telling stories, and encouraging them to escape into a world of imagination and wonder. Some of his most disturbed youngsters he found to be very talented poets, for example. He has always had a wicked sense of humour, which has blossomed only during the time he has spent with his wife, Denise. This sense of humour also allowed many youngsters to survive often difficult and brutalising home environments.

In 2006, he retired after forty years working in schools with young people who had significantly disrupted lives because of behaviour disorders and poor social adjustment, generally brought about through circumstances beyond their control. At the same time as moving from leafy lane suburban middle-class school teaching in Leeds to residential schooling for emotional and behavioural disturbance in the early 1990s, changed family circumstance provided the spur to achieve ambitions. Supported by his wife, Denise, he achieved a Master's degree in his mid-forties and a PhD at the age of fifty-six, because he had always wanted to do so.

Now enjoying glorious retirement, he spends as much time as life will allow writing, reading and travelling.

Other books for adults he has written:

Jack the Lad	Published 2016
Jack	Published 2016
Hit the Road Jack	Published 2017
Welcome Back Jack	Published 2017
All Right Jack?	Published 2019
Carry On Jack	Published 2020
Where to Now, Jack?	Published 2022
Hidden Secrets	Published 2021
Secrets Revealed	Published 2022

Children's books he has written to date:

Magic Parcel: The Awakening	Published June 2010
Magic Parcel: The Gathering Storm	Published March 2011
Magic Parcel: A New Dawn	Published August 2012
18 Mulberry Road	Published September 2011
25 Primrose Walk	Published January 2013
Autumn Adventures	Published September 2013
Winter Tales	Published September 2014
Towards Spring	Published September 2016
Juniper's Tale	Published August 2018
Honey	Published January 2019
The Story of Lemuel Pecker	Published April 2019
Josephine's Journey	Published June 2019
Holly's Prize	Published April 2020

Garnett's Grand Getaway	Published May 2020
Sara's Astonishing Story	Published June 2020
The Boys in Black	Published August 2020
The Magic Whistle and the Tiny Bag of Wishes	Published October 2020
Half Moon Farm	Published March 2021
The Spirit Tree	Published February 2022
Mabel's Miraculous Manner	Published September 2022